"It's Sergeant Thompson. But his face is all wrong."

Gerber slipped into the paddy and rolled Thompson over. The face was distorted from the pressure created by a shot to the back of the head.

The ground in front of the jeep was littered with brass casings, and the vehicle was riddled with bullet holes. A couple of empty magazines lay under the jeep. At the rear was a vacant space where the radio had been. It was obvious. Thompson had been ambushed on the open road.

Gerber checked the body and found the bullet hole. The tattooing around it suggested that the weapon had been only inches from Thompson's head. He had been executed.

"Captain," came Fetterman's voice. "Movement to the right. See that large palm with all the dead leaves? Now, to the right, about ten meters, there's a rusting oil drum."

Gerber stared at the open ground, but saw no movement. A gentle breeze stirred the dead branches of the palm. He suddenly became aware of the heat and humidity, and something else, which he couldn't name. He swallowed. Then he saw it—a streak of khaki as someone dived from the doorway of a hootch to the protection of the rusted oil drum.

"Get ready," hissed Gerber. "They're coming for us."

VIETNAM: GROUND ZERO™

TET

ERIC HELM

A GOLD EAGLE BOOK FROM
WORLDWIDE®

TORONTO · NEW YORK · LONDON · PARIS
AMSTERDAM · STOCKHOLM · HAMBURG
ATHENS · MILAN · TOKYO · SYDNEY

First edition April 1988

ISBN 0-373-62711-4

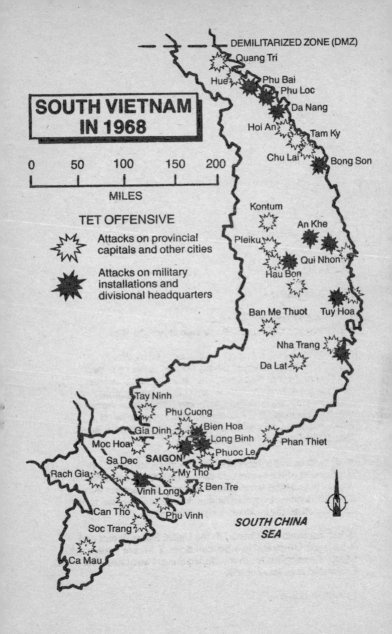

VIETNAM: GROUND ZERO.

PROLOGUE

The funeral service was almost over. From her vantage point at the rear of the temple, Le Tran Duc stood unobtrusively, listening as the priest intoned the final rites. She tried to contain her impatience, wishing the cleric would hurry up and end the service. To take her mind off her restlessness, she let her gaze wander to each family member, finally coming to rest on the sacrificial foods at the front of the altar. In the tropical heat, buzzing flies flitted from sweetmeat to fruit-rice cakes, papaya, mango—then, satisfied, darted to alight on the cover of the coffin, which was closed due to the serious nature of the deceased's injuries.

Soon it was over, and the coffin was borne from the temple and taken to a cemetery in the middle of Saigon. Staying at a discreet distance, Le Tran Duc followed the procession through a wrought-iron gate, up a gentle slope, where the coffin was placed next to the grave near a large tree.

As the funeral party departed, Le Tran Duc remained behind, waiting for the gravediggers to fill the hole. Once again she hung back, this time under the shade of the tree as the men slowly completed their job. When they finished and left the area, Le Tran Duc moved forward and inspected the site. There was nothing unusual about it. Just another grave of a man who had died in an accident recently. At least that was what it might look like to unsuspecting observers. It was one of many she had inspected in the last few weeks.

Le Tran Duc knew better. She knew what was really buried there, having witnessed the contents of the coffin. Her job was over for the time being. She left the grave site quickly, walked through the iron gate and turned once to look back. She was trying to memorize the exact location of the grave, because the next time she saw it it would be dark and there could be people who didn't want her to find it.

She hurried from the cemetery, hailed a cab and climbed in. The driver paid no attention to her. He was angry that he hadn't found an American he could cheat out of a couple of dollars.

Le Tran Duc smiled as they drove into downtown Saigon. The task was finished. At least for a couple of weeks.

1

THE WIRE SERVICE BUREAU, DOWNTOWN SAIGON, JANUARY 19, 1968

Mark Hodges sat in the tiny cubicle off the so-called city room of his wire service bureau, studying the movements of the reporters and photographers who worked with him. Hodges was a short man, and slightly overweight. His black hair, which was usually greased down so that he didn't have to comb it more than once a day, contrasted sharply with his pasty skin, the result of staying indoors most of the time. Hodges hated the tropics, the humidity and the South Vietnamese. He did as much of his work as he could by using the phone and only ventured from the air-conditioned comfort of his office when he couldn't help it.

The office, a concession to his position with the bureau, wasn't as large as those of the correspondents across the hall from the city room, but as a senior editor, he deserved more than a beat-up chair in the city room. His desk was a scarred relic donated by MACV when the generals replaced the worn-out equipment several months earlier, but it was functional. Battleship-gray paint was peeling from it, and one of the file drawers stuck most of the time, so he kept his bottle of bourbon in it. The chair, also from MACV, had an irritating squeak

that Hodges refused to oil because it kept boring people out
of his office. If someone was taking up too much of his time,
he just rocked back and forth until they fled. To the right was
a small bookcase that contained science fiction and mysteries
but nothing that related to Vietnam or the war.

Hodges rocked back, laced his fingers behind his head and
propped his feet on the desk. His shoes suddenly became the
subject of intense scrutiny. Again they were military issue,
shined each night by a maid whose teeth were nearly as black
as his footwear. She was a young, attractive woman whose only
flaw, as far as Hodges was concerned, was her black teeth. If
she kept her mouth shut, he would be willing to overlook it.

He raised his eyes and surveyed the city room spread out in
front of him. Many of the desks were scrounged from the military. The newer desks were near the windows at the front of
the room or on the side opposite Hodges. The longer a reporter had been in Saigon, the closer to the windows he or she
was allowed to move. To his left, along the wall, there were
filing cabinets that contained everything that anyone had been
able to learn about Saigon and its nightlife. But they really held
little of actual importance.

His attention was diverted from the contents of the city room
to Robin Morrow, a photojournalist who stumbled into the big
room and dropped her camera bag on the chair at her desk. It
was one of the few that wasn't gray. Instead, it was an ugly
washed-out green. She leaned a hip against the desk and began sorting through her messages.

Hodges sighed as he stared at her. She was a tall, slender
woman with light brown hair bleached blond by the tropical
sun and green eyes. She wore her standard uniform, which was
a khaki jumpsuit with the legs cut off at midthigh, the sleeves
chopped off and rolled above her elbows. Her hair was cut in
bangs that touched her eyes. For some time now, Hodges
wanted to get close to her, and he had offered her promotions
and hot assignments to do so, but Morrow was too clever to fall
into the trap. Besides, she was seeing, or loved, an officer in
the Special Forces, and he had provided her with a couple of
very good exclusives.

She tossed the messages on her desk and turned to look at Hodges. She smiled and lifted a hand in greeting. That was all the encouragement he needed. He dropped his feet to the floor, grabbed a file folder from his desk and stepped out into the city room.

Morrow saw him coming, moved the camera bag to the floor and sat down. She spun toward him, leaned an elbow on her desk and cupped her chin in her hand, waiting.

Hodges approached, waving the file like a banner. "Got something here for you if you've got nothing else on."

Morrow shrugged. "Nothing that can't wait forever if it has to."

Hodges stopped close to her desk and dropped the file on it. "Group of the local intelligentsia have called for new elections with the National Liberation Front participating."

"Oh, Christ, Mark, get serious."

He shook his head slowly. "Hey, it's what's going on now. Politicians at home falling all over themselves to make Vietnam the big issue in the coming election. Hell, a few days ago a couple of hundred college economists got together to oppose tax increases."

"Who cares what a bunch of college teachers think?"

"I'm not sure that's the point," said Hodges. "I think the point is that the news has been so slow we're interested in what they think because it uses up space in the papers."

Morrow rubbed a hand across her forehead, massaging it as if she had a headache. "Comes to that, does it? We're not interested in the story but only in filling space."

"Now don't start on that, Robin. Anyway, you want to run over to MACV and get someone's reaction to this call for elections? Maybe throw in a couple of questions about the economists. Local reaction to the mood on the American college campuses."

"What is the mood?"

Hodges shrugged. "Hell, I don't know. Opposition to the war. Something like that."

"Aren't you assuming a lot?"

"I'm not assuming anything," countered Hodges. "I'm looking for stories. Everything's winding down here. Number of contacts between our people and the enemy is dropping off. Nothing interesting has happened since the Saigon regime threw Everett Morton out two weeks ago."

"Maybe if you work at it hard enough," Morrow said, smiling, "they'll throw you out, too."

Hodges stood up. "No, I'll never have that kind of luck. I could write that Thieu and Ky were running prostitutes and probably queer for each other and no one would notice."

Morrow shoved her chair back and stood with a sigh. "If you really want me to go over to MACV on this I will, but I'd prefer not to."

"Until someone does something interesting, that's all we're going to get. With the VC and NVA agitating for a truce during Tet, we're not going to see a thing until the middle of February, if then."

Morrow grabbed her camera bag and slipped the strap over her shoulder. "There had better be something of interest over at MACV, or I'm going to be royally pissed."

"Robin! I'm shocked at your language."

"You'll be more than shocked if this is another of those lousy 'let's fill the newspaper with a lot of claptrap about the war so that Johnson and his cronies can look good in the Presidential primaries next month.'"

"Just go over and see what's happening there. If nothing turns up, try the embassy or come back here."

Robin stood for a moment, looking at the rows of empty desks around her, and wondered where in the hell everyone else had gotten to. She raised an eyebrow and pointed.

"They're out looking for stories, but I think this one is about to wrap up. It's all over except for the shouting, and in six months we'll all be in the States telling each other lies about how rough the duty was."

MASTER SERGEANT Anthony B. Fetterman sat in the dayroom at MACV Headquarters, flipping through a copy of *Stars and Stripes* and listening to the rock and roll broadcast on

AFVN. Fetterman was a small man, no more than five-seven, who looked as if he should be hustling pots and pans door-to-door. He had dark skin, baked to the color of mahogany by the tropical sun. His thinning hair was black, and he had a heavy beard that required him to shave twice a day while in Saigon. His jungle fatigues were clean and pressed but not starched, and there was a brush shine on his boots. He looked comfortable and relaxed and not the least bit dangerous, until you saw his eyes. Then he looked like the most dangerous man alive.

He was waiting for Captain MacKenzie K. Gerber, a Special Forces officer who, like Fetterman, was on his second tour in South Vietnam. Gerber was a young man, not much over thirty, tall and slim. Since he had arrived in Vietnam, he had lost weight, like almost everyone else. His brown hair was beginning to show a little gray, and his eyes were blue.

Fetterman turned in his chair, saw that he was alone in the dayroom and turned up the radio. Rock music had to be loud to be appreciated. There was such a blending of sounds and notes that the only way to catch the subtle nuances of the music was to play it loud. Parents, officers and teachers didn't seem to understand that. They just labeled it all noise and condemned it. Fetterman understood why the kids were rebelling on the campuses. If he had been there, he was sure he would have joined them.

As he turned over the last page, having learned that, according to several high-ranking Democrats and more than a few highly placed sources, the war was winding down, he saw Gerber enter. He tapped the paper. "You seen this?"

"No," answered Gerber. "I'm tired of the press and the politicians telling me the war is all but over."

"That mean we have something cooking?"

Gerber dropped into a chair opposite Fetterman. He studied the diminutive sergeant and then the dayroom. A new couch, unscarred end tables, a refrigerator that was humming in the corner, racks of paperbacks with the covers looking clean and a console TV. "The brass sure take care of themselves, don't they?"

"I think this is an NCOs' lounge," responded Fetterman. "We'd never get near anything for the real brass."

"Right," said Gerber, nodding. "You know, this makes me sick. Guys in the field living in rat-infested bunkers who are lucky to get one hot meal a day. Then in Saigon, twelve, twenty miles away, I'll bet there are men who've never been without air-conditioning."

"Yes, sir." Fetterman was getting used to Gerber's philosophical comments. He found that the best course was to ignore them. "We have an assignment?"

"Not much of one, I'm afraid. We're to head over to Duc Hoa and check out the area. Seems there've been some documents uncovered that suggest the district is a hotbed of VC activity."

Fetterman had to smile at that. "Not many places have been a hotbed of anything lately."

Gerber rubbed a hand over his eyes and took a deep breath. "I'm getting very tired of this." He tapped the paper. "According to these clowns, we'll all be home by June."

"That's because the enemy has been defeated and is in hiding," said Fetterman, quoting from the paper.

"I don't think so. I know that's what Johnson and his boys would like to think, but I just don't believe it. There's something brewing."

Fetterman folded the paper and put it on the rack with the latest from *Saigon*, *Time* and *Newsweek*. "Yeah," he said. "Charlie's up to something." He grinned sheepishly and added, "I hate to sound like a bad Western, but it is too quiet. I don't like it."

"Maybe we'll see something at Duc Hoa that'll give us a clue as to what Charlie has in mind."

"Or maybe we'll just see open rice fields and deserted swamps."

MASTER SERGEANT Andy Santini stood at the makeshift gate in the barbed wire and concertina fence that protected the intelligence bunker. The MP, a young man in sweat-stained fatigues and a black helmet liner, examined Santini's ID card and then checked his name against the access list that was prepared each morning. The MP knew Santini well enough to buy him a beer in the club but insisted on seeing his ID anyway. Since the access roster changed daily, he had to consult it.

"Yep," he said, "you're still good." He put the clipboard down and opened the gate. After Santini passed through it, he gave him another clipboard and asked him to sign in. That was in case something happened and there was an inquiry; the investigators would have a written record of who had been around to witness it.

Santini signed his name and glanced at his watch. He added the time and handed the clipboard to the MP. "Thanks."

Santini was a small man, not unlike Fetterman. He had a thin face with a pointed chin and a dark complexion. With his dark eyes and dark hair he looked Latin. He had spent part of his tour in the field, but then had broken an ankle and was given duty at Nha Trang. He had found a niche that he liked and tried to be efficient at his job. Part of it was to stay current on the latest that the intel boys were gathering on a daily basis.

He entered the bunker, a structure created out of wooden beams and sandbags. There was a narrow stairway leading down, and the walls were made of thick boards that bled sap. The size and construction of the bunker gave it a cool interior that was augmented by several small air-conditioning units. Santini walked along a hallway lined with thick doors, some of which contained combination locks.

He stopped in front of one door, was about to knock and then decided against it. Instead, he turned a corner into another dimly lit corridor and walked to the end. There, he knocked and waited. A tiny window opened, a face appeared and then the window shut. A second later the door opened.

"Come on in."

Santini entered the brightly lit room. There were two large tables in the center of it where a corporal and a private worked, plotting suspected enemy locations on maps. Santini noticed that the units being marked were small, platoon-size or company-size, but there seemed to be a lot of them.

At the far end of the room was another thick door, but it stood open, showing the interior of the interrogation rooms. Santini took a step toward it. The gently sloping floor led to a drain at its center. The walls were covered with thick padding, and there was a single light bulb dangling from an exposed wire. Two klieg lights on tripods stood near one wall, their power cords trailing into the map room.

There was a lone figure in the center of the room, her chair sitting above the drain. She was wearing black shorts and nothing else. Her hands were tied behind her, with one end of the rope reaching down for the crosspiece of the chair so that her shoulders were drawn back and lifted. Her feet were spread and tied to the legs of the chair so that her bottom rested on the front edge. It gave her an unnatural and uncomfortable posture.

"What's going on?" asked Santini.

"Vietcong," said the sergeant who had let Santini in. "Caught her trying to sneak onto the base this morning with a load of explosives."

Santini stepped forward so that he could see more. There were two Vietnamese in the room and one American. The American stood to the side, his eyes on the light bulb.

One of the Vietnamese shoved his face into that of the woman and shouted something at her. The speech was too fast for Santini to understand any of it. The woman turned her head so that she didn't have to look at her interrogator. He reached out and grabbed her chin, forcing her to stare into his eyes.

"They got anything from her?" asked Santini.

"Nothing of interest. She claims a man asked her to carry the bag into the camp. She says she didn't think anything of it and didn't bother to look into it."

"That's a real possibility," said Santini.

"I'd be inclined to agree with you," said the sergeant, "except she's not a regular member of the work force. This is the first time anyone remembers seeing her."

There was a wet slap and a scream. Santini turned and saw that a red welt had risen on the bare skin of the woman. The Vietnamese now held a length of bamboo. He shouted at the woman, and when she didn't respond fast enough, he punched her in the stomach. She jerked against her bonds and moaned.

"Say," said Santini, suddenly sickened. "Isn't this going too far? There's no need for this."

"Vietnamese can do anything they want. If we complain, we're told to let the Vietnamese handle their own problems and stay out of it."

There was another scream. Santini saw the Vietnamese raise the bamboo over his head, bringing it down rapidly on the woman's chest, abdomen and shoulders. She rocked in the chair, trying to avoid the blows. Blood spattered the floor as the man attacked her thighs.

Santini leaped forward, but before he could do anything, the second Vietnamese soldier grabbed the arm of the first. He spun him away from his victim and then shoved him toward the door, shouting at the man and pushing him into the map room. As the two men entered, the second grinned at the first. Santini realized it was the old Mutt and Jeff routine. One interrogator is the bad guy, cruel and unreasonable. The second is kind, pretending to be on the side of the victim. It was a trick so old that it had whiskers, and Santini couldn't believe anyone would still fall for it.

The second man returned to the room where the woman was sobbing almost hysterically. Her chin nearly touched her chest, and there was sweat glistening on her body. The man crouched next to her and gently lifted her face, speaking softly. He talked to her, nodded at the door and then shook his head.

Santini couldn't hear what was being said, but he could figure it out. She was being told that the first man wanted to kill her slowly, with as much pain as possible. He hated the Vietcong and wanted them all dead. The second man was saying he understood that mistakes could be made. People sometimes didn't understand the consequences of their actions. He would protect her. He would see that she was taken to the POW compound, given food and medical aid and treated with human dignity. But he needed something to prove that she was willing to cooperate, some information to show her good faith. If she did that, then he could protect her. If not, who knew what could happen?

The woman didn't speak. She continued to cry, her shoulders shaking. The second interrogator snapped his fingers and held out his hand. The American handed him a wet cloth, which he used to wipe some of the blood from her body and then dabbed at her face, cleaning it.

She mumbled something and the man nodded. He spoke rapidly and then shouted into the map room. The interrogator there grinned, then left the room.

"Looks like she's going to talk."

Santini moved to the right and pulled out a chair. He dropped into it, realizing how sick he felt. He was light-headed and couldn't seem to focus on anything. The problem was that he didn't like torture, no matter what the reasons. He believed in the rules of land warfare. Soldiers should be questioned but not tortured. There were many conflicting emotions running through him.

A moment later the American appeared in the doorway and announced, "She's not the first to bring munitions onto the base here. I want someone to contact the provost marshal and alert him. Ask him if he could swing by here so we can brief him."

Santini stood and stepped close to the man. "What'd she tell you?"

"Just that there's a raid planned to hit us sometime in the next few days. She isn't sure when."

Santini looked beyond the MP. The woman was slumped in the chair. Her feet had been freed and the rope linking her wrists to the back rung of the chair had been loosened, but her hands were still bound behind her.

"She tell you anything else?"

"Not yet. I think there's some more to learn. I think we'll get it in a few minutes. She's talking now."

"Yeah," said Santini. "I see that."

CAPTAIN JONATHAN BROMHEAD stood near the smoking ruins of a rearm bunker and shook his head. Bromhead was nearing his twenty-seventh birthday, but still looked as if he belonged in high school. He was a freckle-faced kid with light hair that turned coppery in a certain light. Tall and slender, he had been the exec of an A-Detachment on his first tour in Vietnam and had lucked into command of one for his second. Many of the men on second and third tours had been diverted to MACV-SOG or Project Delta.

Bromhead turned to Sergeant First Class Tyme, a tall sandy-haired man nearing thirty whose love of weapons was all-consuming. When Bromhead had found himself with a hole in his detachment, he had asked that Sergeant Tyme join him. In the few months that they had worked the assignment together, Bromhead had never regretted the decision, but then they had served together on their first tours, so Bromhead had known that Tyme was a top-notch soldier.

"How long to replace it?" asked Bromhead.

Tyme crouched and reached out, pushing a partially burned sandbag out of the way. "There wasn't much of interest in there, Captain. Just spare ammo, a few weapons and some boxes of grenades. Paperwork'll take a couple of hours, and then if I hand-carry it to Saigon, I should have the stuff back by nightfall." Tyme suddenly realized he had talked himself out of a night in Saigon, and he amended his original statement. "Midmorning tomorrow at the latest."

Bromhead smiled. "You sure about that? Couldn't have it accomplished this afternoon?"

Tyme turned to look up into the captain's eyes. "You think there's going to be a problem?"

Bromhead glanced around. There was a squad of Vietnamese working on the wire, restringing some of it, adding tanglefoot and attaching more empty cans to the concertina. Another group, led by Sergeant Ashly, was checking the claymore mines, making sure that VC sappers hadn't sneaked in during the night and turned them around as they sometimes did. A third party was making a final weapons check before heading out to search the jungle near the camp. No one was standing close to them.

"Justin, I don't like any of this. Charlie has been lying low too long. I think something is building and Charlie is afraid of tipping his hand if he's not careful. I think he's being too careful. We should be extra cautious."

"Okay, sir," Tyme said seriously. He knew that Bromhead could sense things. The young captain seemed to see things on a subliminal level and used that to form his opinions. He had called the mortar attack the night before on the button. He'd told the team at the evening meal that he thought they would take a half-dozen mortar rounds about three in the morning. It had been ten at two forty-five.

"I can have the requisitions ready in an hour and catch the morning chopper to Cu Chi. Then on to Saigon, and if you'll grease the skids, I can be back by midafternoon."

"I'm sorry, Justin," Bromhead said. "I know I should let you have the night in Saigon, but I'd really prefer that you were here tonight. If it doesn't happen today, it will sometime in the next week or so."

Tyme stood and clapped his hands together, brushing the dirt from them. He wiped the back of his hand across his lips. "Tet is coming up. Charlie's making a big stink about a cease-fire during the holidays. Claims he's going to observe it even if the running dog Americans don't."

Bromhead grinned. "And you believe that?"

"Yes, sir. That and in the Easter bunny and the three little pigs."

"Okay," said Bromhead. He turned and started walking toward the team house. Tyme fell in beside him. "Tell you what. You get the papers ready and get out of here. I'll call and see if I can't get the ammo delivered over to Tan Son Nhut so that you don't have to go chasing around for it. That should give you some time to fool around in Saigon. At the very least, you'll be able to hit the PX, drink a beer in the club and chase a couple of Vietnamese girls."

"Thanks, sir."

LE TRAN DUC BRUSHED her long black hair back, away from her face, and stared into the bright tropical light of downtown Saigon. She was a tall Eurasian woman whose father, a French soldier, had fought the Viet Minh. But she hated Westerners with a passion. It was her belief that the father who had lived with her and her mother for three years had deserted them when the French had been defeated at Dien Bien Phu. Their lives from that point had been one of hardship, her mother forced into prostitution and both of them despised by other Vietnamese.

A woman with fine features, high cheekbones and large brown eyes, she was chased by men of all ranks. Most of the time she ignored the advances. Occasionally she turned on soldiers to tantalize them, and sometimes she responded favorably to those with high ranks or jobs in the embassy.

She sat in a small café, wearing the hated dress of a Western woman, her skirt to midthigh and her blouse molded to her upper body. Across the street was the gate to the embassy, and she watched to see how the guards reacted to the situations thrown at them. She wrote nothing down, memorizing the times and locations of the soldiers and sipping the tea that a young Vietnamese man bought for her.

When two Marines from the embassy guard force, now off-duty, entered, she smiled at them and then lowered her eyes. The cultured Vietnamese woman didn't flirt openly with men, especially Westerners, but she knew they had noticed her.

The Marines ordered tea and then took it to a table close to Le Tran. They tried to watch her without her knowing it. She played them like game fish, giving them a little line and then snapping the hook tight.

Slowly she crossed her legs, noticing their eyes dip. She leaned back, lifted her hands and ran them through her long hair. As she moved, the blouse was stretched across her breasts. When they were staring at her chest, she uncrossed her legs, kept her knees apart and watched them try to bore holes in her thighs.

One of them stood, turned his back and pulled at his uniform. He spun toward her and began walking toward her table. Before he could get close to her, the young Vietnamese man who had been standing at the back of the café came forward carrying two cups of tea. He sat down with Le Tran before the American could get too close.

Le Tran smiled at him and then shook her head slightly, as if telling the American that he hadn't moved fast enough. The Marine returned to his friend and said loudly, ''Fucking tease.''

2

MACV HEADQUARTERS
SAIGON

Brigadier General Thomas Harkin sat behind his huge rose-wood desk and studied the report in front of him. As he read, he fiddled with the pen from a gold set, occasionally tapping it on the green felt blotter. A fancy clock with an inscription sat next to a small lamp that cast a pool of light on the sheet of paper Harkin was reading. His starched and pressed jungle fatigues showed no sign of wear, no sign of harsh laundering, and no sweat stains.

Standing at attention on a small woven rug before Harkin was Major Richard Hobbs. He was a stout man whose light skin rejected the tanning of a tropical sun so that he was a pumpkin color when he wasn't peeling. His thinning blond hair didn't protect his head from the sun, so he was one of the few men who never neglected to wear a hat outside.

Harkin flipped over the last page of the report, then looked up at Hobbs. "Okay. I think I have the picture now. What I want you to do is downplay all this for the press conference."

"Downplay it?"

"That's right. Official word from Washington through the embassy here is that the war is winding down. The enemy is no longer capable of launching any attacks other than small mortar and rocket harassments designed to obtain press interest.''

Hobbs took a step forward and reached for the report. ''But, General, we have information that the enemy is massing his forces in the area.''

''I know that. I can read just as well as you can. And I know about the attack on Plei Soi. All that makes no difference.'' Harkin grinned broadly. ''You have to remember that this is an election year. Congressional and senate seats up for grabs. A Presidential election. Bad press from here could sink more than a few campaigns.''

''How is misleading the press going to help?''

''Now wait a minute, Major. No one said a word about misleading the press. You provide the information for them and answer their questions. Just don't volunteer any information.''

''Yes, sir.''

''If they ask, tell them that the enemy is in the process of rebuilding. There's a lull in the fighting. You expect something to happen.''

''Yes, sir.''

''Just a couple of weeks ago General Westmoreland predicted a major enemy offensive in the near future.'' Harkin chuckled. ''That made him no friends in Washington, but then the press ignored his statement anyway. We play it honest with them, but we don't have to hand them everything.''

''I understand.''

''Good. Now I'll want a full report just as soon as you've completed your press conference.''

Hobbs came to stiff attention and saluted. He spun and stepped to the door. As he walked through the outer office and entered the corridor, he realized he was the sacrificial lamb. If anything went wrong, if a lot of unfavorable stories appeared in the hometown newspapers it was his head that would roll. That was why he had inherited the job of briefing the press. Harkin and the others considered him expendable. Unlike them, he couldn't delegate the job, because if his captain or sergeant blew it, the general would still fire him.

He stopped outside the door of the pressroom. With a hand on the knob, he took a deep breath. He touched his face with the sleeve of his jungle fatigues, blotting up the sweat that even three tons of air-conditioning on the building's roof couldn't stop, and then threw open the door.

The members of the media were standing in small groups, talking to one another when Hobbs opened the door. As he entered, they looked up and fell silent, then began moving toward their seats. Hobbs noticed that even though seats hadn't been assigned, a natural pecking order had been established. The wire services, TV networks and major newspapers representatives were in the front. In the rear were the free-lancers and small newspapers like the *Des Moines Register* or the *Kansas City Star*.

Hobbs moved to the raised stage and set his notes on the lectern. "I have a brief statement and then I'll take your questions."

He waited for a moment, but no one objected. "In the past twenty-four hours there have been fourteen mortar and rocket attacks directed against our bases. These attacks were small-scale and scattered throughout all of South Vietnam. As of now, we have no indications that there were any casualties, and the damage to U.S. facilities and equipment was light."

He flipped over a page and continued. "Current estimates place the number of enemy soldiers in South Vietnam, and this figure includes NVA, Vietcong and irregular forces, at around three hundred thousand. That's a slight increase over last month's figures."

Hobbs again waited for a response and again was disappointed. He concluded his briefing by saying, "Finally, we have a report that the North Vietnamese and the Pathet Lao overran the town of Nambac about sixty miles from the royal capital of Luang Prabang. Now are there any questions?"

A man stood but didn't identify himself. "Would it be fair to assume that the current trend will last through the lunar new year?"

"We're not sure how long the trend will last. Naturally we're trying to assess the situation."

"Which is another way of saying you don't know."

"It means, sir," said Hobbs, "that we're watching the enemy. Right now he's avoiding a fight and has seriously stepped down the number of mortar attacks launched. It's a trend that will continue for another few days."

"Has there been any discussion about withdrawing American forces from Vietnam now that the enemy is pulling back?"

Hobbs stared at the woman who had asked the question. She was large and stout and wrapped in sufficient khaki to make several pup tents. He hesitated before answering because he could still hear Harkin telling him that the politicians were worried. The perfect opportunity to mislead the press had just surfaced. They had made a false assumption based on incomplete information. But he knew that it would come back to haunt him if he didn't handle it just right.

"There have been no discussions about a reduction in the size of the American commitment to Vietnam. What we have is a lull in the fighting, and we expect an upswing."

"Could you clarify that?" shouted a man in the back.

"There's really nothing to clarify. The enemy is taking a break right now—"

"Then you expect a general battle to develop?"

Hobbs turned and stared at the man standing in the middle of the room. A tall, thin man with graying hair. Hobbs shook his head. "No. I have no expectations. I'm merely reporting the observations made at this time. Enemy activity has been significantly reduced."

"There is talk," said another man, "that the war will be over in six months."

"I would see that as optimistic," said Hobbs. He then wished he had bitten his tongue.

"Could you give us your opinion about the possible conclusion of the war?" the same man asked.

Hobbs glanced at his notes, but there was nothing there that could help him. He stepped to the side of the lectern and leaned an elbow on it.

"I'm only a major," he said, stalling. "I have no opinions about the end of the war. Observed fact is that the enemy isn't initiating large-scale actions now. We've been pursuing the enemy and have had little luck. The last major battle, if you want to call it that, was at Plei Soi. The enemy force there was beaten off.''

"The general tone," said the tall gray-haired man, "is that the enemy is avoiding a fight."

"That is correct."

"Then the assumption would be that the enemy is defeated. He's fighting a rearguard action, hoping for the best terms at the negotiating table."

"I would think that you might be reading too much into this lull," said Hobbs.

Again he wished he had kept his mouth shut. The reporters had made their assumptions and were driving toward them, and he was doing everything he could to dissuade them. It wasn't what he had been told to do.

"Is it fair," asked the gray-haired man, "to assume that the South Vietnamese will be taking a greater role in the fighting of the war?"

"Yes," said Hobbs.

"And is it fair to say that the enemy forces have failed to gain any significant victories in a number of months?"

"Yes," said Hobbs, nodding slowly.

"Then, wouldn't you suspect that American troop reductions would begin soon, that the war is nearly over?"

Hobbs looked at the floor. This was exactly the impression he was supposed to leave with the press. They had done everything to bring about these conclusions themselves, ignoring his reminders that the enemy was still out there. The press wanted to believe the war was almost over. But it was an impression Hobbs didn't want to convey.

"I would say that such a conclusion may be premature."

The newsman nodded knowingly. Hobbs hadn't denied his conclusion; he had only suggested it was premature. "Thank you, Major."

Hobbs watched them exit and knew what they would write. They had come into the briefing with their conclusions already drawn. If he had been more dishonest, he could have easily led them down the primrose path. As it was, they had to take that route themselves.

GERBER STOOD at the front window of the terminal under the tower at Hotel Three, studying the helicopters as they maneuvered among the concrete pads and the grassy strip near the chain-link fence. The soft boonie hat of one soldier was sucked up in the rotor wash, whipped through the rotor system and thrown into the air. It landed on the far side of the fence where the man couldn't get at it.

Gerber turned. "We can probably catch a hot lunch at Duc Hoa."

"I'm not worried about it," said Fetterman.

"Yeah. You know anyone there?"

Fetterman shook his head. "It's not like the old days where if you didn't know the man, you knew of him. Too many people coming in now. I didn't recognize one name on the roster."

"Well, we'll just have to play it by ear, I'm afraid."

At that moment a man wearing jungle fatigues and an Old West-style holster entered. He stood at the door, surveying the crowd, and then shouted, "Anyone needing a ride to Duc Hoa, Duc Hue or Cu Chi, I'm getting ready for takeoff."

Gerber leaned over and grabbed his pack. He hadn't brought much more than his canteens, first-aid kit, combat knife and a clean pair of socks. He figured that if he was going to be at Duc Hoa for a couple of days, he could beg, borrow or steal anything else he needed. He also had a bandolier of ammo for his M-16 because he believed that he could never have enough ammo, contrary to what the Army seemed to think.

Gerber waited until Fetterman shrugged into his pack. Fetterman always carried more than he needed. He had learned his lessons in World War II where the supply bases had often been a hundred miles to the rear with no easy way to get to them. It was always better to have too much than too little. Even the air mobility of Vietnam hadn't broken Fetterman of the habit.

Together they walked out onto the helipad. There was a blast of hot wind as another helicopter took off. Fetterman grabbed at his hat to keep from losing it. Gerber ducked his head, tucking in his chin, and closed his eyes. When the chopper was gone, he opened them and continued to the aircraft.

They climbed into the cargo compartment and sat down on the troop seat. Since it was only a routine flight, and not a combat assault, Gerber buckled his seat belt. He set the butt of his weapon on the floor, the muzzle pointed toward the top of the cargo compartment.

A moment later they were joined by three other men. Two of them wore old, stained and frayed jungle fatigues. The other had on a bright green uniform that contained no insignia. He had two duffel bags stuffed with equipment, which were shoved against the pilots' seats. He sat on the floor between them, facing Gerber and Fetterman.

"You new in-country?" asked Fetterman.

"Been here almost four days now," said the man.

"Only 361 to go."

"Thanks for reminding me."

The pilot strapped himself in, then flipped a couple of switches. He looked out the door and shouted, "Clear!"

The crew chief stood outside the aircraft, a fire extinguisher in his hand, looking in at the engine deck. He shouted "Clear!" back at the pilot.

There was a high-pitched whine that grew in intensity and then was joined by the roar of the turbine engine. The noise grew until it dominated everything around it. Gerber could no longer hear anything that Fetterman said unless the master sergeant leaned close and shouted.

The crew chief fastened the fire extinguisher into its place on the post behind the pilot and then crawled into his well. He leaned out, held a thumb up and the aircraft picked up to a hover. They climbed out then, turning away from Tan Son Nhut and leaving Saigon behind them. In all his time in Vietnam, Gerber couldn't remember ever flying over the city.

Spread out in front of him was the deep green of South Vietnam. There were open fields, rice paddies and clumps of palm and coconut trees. Hidden in some of them were hootches or groups of hootches. They finally crossed Highway One, the link between Saigon and Tay Ninh that eventually reached Phnom Penh. The highway was filled with American convoys of trucks and jeeps, farmers with their oxcarts, Lambrettas carrying passengers, and even a few cars.

South of the highway they crossed a vast swamp that was a free-fire zone. Anyone found inside it was considered the enemy and taken under fire. They flew over the wreckage of a South Vietnamese A-1E Skyraider shot down weeks earlier.

Coming up on Duc Hoa from the north, they circled to the south near the Song Vam Co Dong and approached the runway inside the wire. The helicopter flared, and Gerber lost sight of everything except the cloudless blue sky. As the pilot leveled the skids, slowing, the rotor wash splashed against the red dust of the crushed gravel runway, blowing outward. They touched down next to a giant pond in the middle of the camp. On the other side were several concrete pads, which served as a refueling point for helicopters.

Gerber rose from the troop seat, crouched and stepped toward the open door of the cargo compartment. He dropped to the ground. When Fetterman joined him, they jogged to the side and then turned. The chopper picked up to a hover, the rotor wash kicking up a cloud of red dust and swirling debris.

As the chopper crossed the wire and turned back to the west, Fetterman asked, "Now what?"

Gerber turned, taking it all in: the bunkers of green rubberized sandbags at the corners of the perimeter; the strands of barbed wire and concertina; the small bunkers scattered around, guarding the approaches to the airstrip. Behind him, beyond the pond that looked like a dumping ground, he could see the buildings of Duc Hoa. The map he had checked had indicated a plantation, but he saw none of the structures that suggested it was. And although there were men working around the perimeter, and in the bunkers, no one was rushing out to meet them.

"Guess we better go find the reception committee," said Gerber.

Fetterman shouldered his gear. "Right behind you, Captain."

They skirted the edge of the pool and walked through a gate in the wire. As they entered the compound proper, a man came rushing toward them. He was a tall, heavy man with thick black hair covering his bare chest and shoulders. Sweat glistened in it, suggesting he had been on a work detail. When he slid to a halt close to them, the sweat stains around the waist of his jungle pants were obvious. The knees were stained red from the dirt of the compound, and his boots might have originally been red, since there wasn't a trace of black on them.

"Can I help you, sir?" he asked, raising a hand to his head. He wasn't saluting, just shading his eyes.

Gerber nodded. "Sergeant Fetterman and I flew in from Saigon to check out some rumors that Charlie thinks of this area as home."

The expression on the man's face changed immediately, as if a nerve had been struck. He lowered his hand as his eyes hardened. "We've heard that rumor, too."

"Yes, well," said Gerber rubbing his jaw, "here's the deal. We're getting a little concerned about all these rumors of the VC around but no one seeing them. We've come to see for ourselves."

"Yes, sir."

"Your team commander around?"

"Captain Jewell is in the commo bunker, I believe."

"Sergeant," said Gerber, guessing at the man's rank, since he wasn't wearing a shirt, "this isn't an official visit, nor are we suggesting you're derelict in your duties. We've got reason to believe something is building up, and we want to check it out. This seemed like a good place for us to do it."

"Yes, sir. If you'll follow me."

As the man turned and began walking away, Fetterman moved close to Gerber and whispered, "He's a little touchy."

"Can't blame him."

They crossed the compound and descended into the darkness of the commo bunker. It looked, felt and smelled like a dozen others: a short flight of steps into a cool interior and a musty, dirty smell hanging in the air. In one corner was a stack of radios, their lights glowing brightly in the dimness. There was a table near them where a man worked in a pool of bright light. He turned as everyone entered.

"What's all this, Albright?"

"Couple of men in from Saigon on some kind of mission."

The man at the map stood and held out his hand. "I'm Captain Jewell. What can I do for you?"

"Sergeant Fetterman and I flew in from Saigon. We've gotten rumblings that something is building up around Saigon, and we wanted a chance to check it out."

"Uh-huh," said Jewell. "Just what have you heard?"

Gerber noticed that the atmosphere in the bunker had suddenly turned icy. Jewell hadn't offered them a seat or asked if they would like something to drink. He was being cautious. Gerber set his weapon on the floor, resting it against the table so that it wouldn't get dirty.

"Captain," he said, "I know what you're thinking, but it's not like that. We came here just to use it as a base of operations while we check out the information. I'd like to take a look at the marketplaces around here, survey the surrounding territory and see what I can see. I'll need your help because I'll want to know if there are suddenly more young men in the fields than there have been. I'll need someone to tell me if the markets are suddenly quieter. There's so much that I need to know if I'm going to make an accurate guess."

Jewell nodded and then ran a hand through his thick hair. He dropped back into his chair and rested his hands in the pool of light on the map. "Please," he said, "have a seat. You have no orders from Saigon?"

"None whatsoever," said Gerber. "We're here to look for the enemy and not to look at your operation. We don't have a lot of time because I think it's going to blow up in our faces."

"Okay, Captain," said Jewell, spinning the map around so that Gerber could see it. "What I've been doing here is consolidating the reports handed in by my intel NCO—the little things that he's noticed in the past week."

Gerber raised his eyebrows and shot a glance at Fetterman. "Such as?"

"As you mentioned before—too many young men in the fields around here." Now Jewell grinned broadly. "Young men with perfect papers."

"Yeah," said Fetterman. "Rice farmers don't have papers because they lose them, but the bad guys always have brand-new ones."

"Exactly. And they don't like going to bed at dusk, so we see signs of lights at night. Music drifts across the rice paddies to us. There've been a couple of complaints of sexual molestation to the local police authorities." Jewell hesitated and added quickly, "One of the men is working for us and told us that. He said that the local headmen have moved to keep the police out of it. They wanted it settled between the girl and the boy."

Gerber nodded.

"Normally, if it was a local boy, it would never have gotten that far. It means the boy, or boys, aren't from around here."

"Okay," said Gerber. "I think I see. You've noticed exactly what we're looking for. Now would it be possible for us to check on this?"

"Sure, I'll assign you a jeep and a driver who's familiar with the area. That do?"

"I don't know about that, Captain," said Fetterman.

"It's no problem," said Jewell. "Our guys drive all over the countryside without trouble. The key is to stay on the main drags and near the people. Be back by five and you won't have any trouble."

"Seems pretty haphazard," commented Fetterman.

"May be, Sergeant, but we've been doing it for months and we haven't had any trouble."

"Then that's what we'd like to do," said Gerber. "We don't want to draw any attention to ourselves. We just want to get a reading on the situation."

Jewell nodded, looking at his watch. "I can have the whole thing laid on for right after lunch. Albright, or one of the others, can drive you around and let you see for yourselves."

"Good," said Gerber. "That's what we want."

3

A TINY CAFE ACROSS
FROM THE AMERICAN
EMBASSY, SAIGON

For nearly two hours Le Tran Duc sat in the café watching the two Marines who had become permanent fixtures. They talked to each other quietly, their eyes shifting to her frequently as she continued to tease them. Occasionally she leaned forward across the table and spoke quietly to the Vietnamese man with her. She wasn't making small talk or telling him how fascinating she found him; she was giving him information about her observations of the American guard force at the embassy and how many times the Vietnamese police drove by.

Finally she said, "Why don't you go take a long walk?"

He nodded and scratched his cheek. "You think it's time?"

"I think our friends are very frustrated now. Yes, I think it's time."

"All right." Sliding back his chair, he stood and bent toward her as if to kiss her lips, but she turned her head so that he merely brushed her cheek.

Without a word, he turned and left the café. Almost before the door had closed, the older of the Marines was on his feet. He moved across the floor with the confidence of an invasion force hitting the beach. Stopping close to the woman, he looked down at her legs, as if judging them for a contest.

Le Tran shifted in her chair. "Yes?"

The Marine took that for an invitation. He appropriated the chair deserted by the Vietnamese man and sat down. Bending forward, his eyes on her thighs, he said, "I couldn't help noticing you." He reached out and touched her knee.

Le Tran smiled slyly. "I noticed that you were noticing. I think I like that."

The Marine was taken slightly aback by her boldness. He sat up straight, appraising her. Then he motioned the Vietnamese woman who was standing near the back wall of the café. "Another tea, please."

"You are a Marine?" asked Le Tran.

"Yes." He pointed through the window at the embassy. "I work over there."

She lowered her eyes, as if impressed. "It must be an important job."

"One of the most important." He stopped talking when the waitress brought his order. Digging into his pockets, he pulled out a wad of bills. Carefully he separated the MPC from the piasters, and handed over a dollar.

"What is your name?" asked Le Tran when the waitress walked away.

"I'm James Lockridge. Jim to my friends."

She held her delicate hand over the table so that it could be shaken in a Western manner. "Hello, Jim," she said. "I am Le Tran Duc."

"Do they call you Le?"

"You may, if you like."

The other Marine, who had been watching the exchange with interest, stood and came over. He slipped into one of the other chairs. "Hi. I'm Franklin Jones."

"Franklin," said Le Tran.

For a moment there was silence as each of them tried to think of something witty to say. Le Tran broke in with, "When do you have to go back to work?"

"Back on duty," corrected Lockridge. "We go back on duty. But not before tomorrow at seven."

"Then you have all afternoon and this evening to spend with me," she said.

Lockridge grinned at Jones. "We certainly do." He slipped his chair closer to her and stole another glance at her thighs. He was certain he could see red panties.

She touched his hand. "I suppose you have got to work harder with Tet coming so soon."

"Naw," said Lockridge. "The slo. . . uh, the Vietnamese have arranged for some kind of cease-fire during Tet. Our CO is trying to arrange it so that we have a fairly light schedule during the holidays. Let us all take advantage of the situation."

"Jim," said Jones, slightly annoyed.

"What?" asked Lockridge. "I'm not saying anything." He patted Le Tran's hand and said, "Frank seems to think that everyone we run into is a spy for the Vietcong. He sees the Communists hiding under his bed at night."

Le Tran pretended surprise. "Is this true?"

"No," responded Jones. "It's just. . . well, we're not supposed to be discussing the details of our jobs with anyone outside the Corps."

Le Tran lifted her eyebrows innocently and gestured at herself. "But surely you do not suspect me of being one so evil? I am just a girl."

Now Jones was stuck. He wasn't sure how to tactfully handle the situation. He shook his head and smiled weakly. "Well, we're supposed to suspect everyone."

"My, it must be awful to have to suspect everyone. When do you have fun?"

"Frank never has fun," said Lockridge. "He just sits around his room studying the manual on being a good NCO and sends in applications for Officer Candidate School."

"Yes," said Le Tran, "you want to be an officer? You must be very clever."

"Say," interrupted Lockridge, not liking the way the conversation had turned, "could you find a friend for Frank?

Then all of us could go out on the town tonight. Eat some dinner, drink, and maybe dance."

"I do not know," said Le Tran. "It might be difficult to find someone so quickly. If you would like to come home with me, my sister who is older than me, might like to have dinner with Frank."

"Hey," said Lockridge, clapping his hands together. "That's great. We'll have a good time."

"Yes," agreed Le Tran, uncrossing her legs slowly so that Lockridge could have a good view of her panties. She stood and took his hand, almost lifting him to his feet. "Please. You both come with me and we will see if my sister would like to have a good dinner tonight."

Got you, Le Tran thought, as they moved toward the door. And it was so easy, too.

TYME STOOD TO THE SIDE of the helipad, watched the chopper settle toward it and kick up a cloud of swirling red dust and then turned his head as the gusts became a hurricane. When the wind diminished and the roar of the engine dropped off, he looked up again. The crew chief was shoving cartons from the cargo compartment, letting them fall to the dirt.

"Say," he called out, "you want to lend a hand here?"

Tyme moved forward. "What do you need?"

"Just help me out so we can get out of here," said the man.

"I'll help unload, but I need a ride to Saigon."

"We're not going to Saigon. We're going to Tay Ninh."

"That'll be fine," said Tyme as he grabbed a box and lifted it. "I can catch a ride to Saigon from there."

"Who's responsible for this stuff?" asked the crew chief.

"If you'll wait a moment, I'll get either Captain Bromhead or Lieutenant Mildebrandt for you."

"That'll be fine."

Tyme grabbed the orange sack that held the mail, both official and personal. He didn't want to let go of it. Instead, he wanted to paw through it, and grab what was his so that he could read it on the chopper, but he knew Captain Bromhead would be annoyed. The captain was a stickler for detail, even when the details didn't make a whole lot of sense.

As he turned to add the sack to the pile of supplies, Mildebrandt appeared at the gate, walking slowly toward them. Mildebrandt was a big man, probably six-three and weighing close to three hundred pounds. There wasn't a sign of fat on him. He had short jet-black hair, light eyes and a Roman nose. The fatigue shirt he wore was stained with sweat under the arms and down the front, though he pretended not to notice the heat or the humidity.

When he was close, he yelled over the roar of the engine, "What all we got?"

"Supplies and the mail." Tyme hesitated and then asked, "I don't suppose you could dig mine out before I take off?"

Mildebrandt looked at him for a moment. "You're getting a trip into Saigon. I'd have thought you wouldn't be worried about the mail."

"Sir?"

Mildebrandt bent over and snagged the bag. He broke the seal, searched through it and handed three letters to Tyme. "I've just gotten myself in trouble with the captain."

"Thanks, sir."

"If you're coming with us," said the crew chief, "you'd better get on board."

Tyme climbed onto the chopper and sat down on the red troop seat. He studied the postmarks on his letters, and put them in the order they'd been written. Then he stuffed two of them into his pocket and ripped open the first.

As he pulled the letter from the envelope, he almost lost the enclosed photo. He turned it over and saw Sara in the smallest bikini he had ever laid eyes on. She was standing on a beach, the water behind her, one shapely leg bent at the knee. She was waving at the camera, a smile on her face. Her long blond hair was pushed behind her shoulders. Tyme wished he was with her. He touched the picture gently, as if he could feel her through the thin paper.

Ignoring the stories of her activities, he read the letter quickly, looking to see if she still missed him and still loved him. Satisfied that she did, he read the letter slowly and then carefully put it into his pocket.

He read the other two letters over and then read each of them carefully a third time, looking for things between the lines, hints that she was tiring of the long-distance affair. But she seemed to care deeply for him. Happily he put the letters into his pocket and then leaned back against the gray soundproofing of the transmission wall of the Huey. He closed his eyes and thought about his last night in the World, the one Sara had promised would be special because he would be gone for a year.

Tyme was completely relaxed, almost asleep. With part of his mind he could hear the steady hum of the engine and the constant pop of the rotors. The air, even at three thousand feet, was heavy with heat and humidity, but it was cooler than it had been on the ground. He opened his eyes once but couldn't see anything except blue sky and a few scattered clouds through the windshield.

In the distance he heard the ripping of cloth and recognized the sound as a burst from an RPD. He glanced to the left, where the sound had come from, and saw a line of tracers flash past. He jerked upright, the blood hammering in his ears and his heart pounding in his chest. He blinked rapidly, turning to the right so that he could try to spot the enemy.

The crew chief to his left opened fire with his M-60 machine gun, the weapon chattering as the belt fed through it. The muzzle-flash was nearly lost in the brightness of the late-morning sun.

The chopper banked, and from far away, just barely penetrating the noise from the helicopter's engine and rotor, Tyme heard the enemy machine gun firing again. The copilot looked over his seat at Tyme and then turned his attention back to the instrument panel.

There was a snapping behind him, and then Tyme felt the aircraft vibrate. He glanced at the front of the Huey and saw the windshield disintegrate into splinters as the bullets from the enemy weapon slammed into it. Sparks cascaded from the circuit breaker panel overhead and smoke began pouring out. The pilot broke to the right, away from the enemy machine gun position. Over the noise Tyme heard someone shout, as if the intercom no longer worked.

The crew chief stopped firing and reached around from his well, grabbing at the sleeve of Tyme's fatigues. He pushed the boom mike out of the way and shouted, "We're going down. Buckle your seat belt."

Tyme dropped onto the red troop seat and fastened the seat belt. He wished he had brought his steel pot instead of his green beret. His knuckles turned white as he clutched his weapon and the chopper fell out of the sky. As the ground rushed up toward him, he hoped that the pilots knew what they were doing. He told himself to trust in their skill, since the training for pilots was one of the longest the Army had. But he also knew that the standards were dropping.

Suddenly the noise from the engine ceased, and the pilot slammed down the collective. Then they rocked back, as if the aircraft was trying to throw them off its back. Only sky and clouds were visible through the windshield. Out the cargo compartment doors was the deep green of the jungle rushing up to meet them. Tyme felt the air change from the almost cool and pleasant atmosphere experienced with altitude to the damp, wet, heat of the jungle.

Then the aircraft leveled, and he saw the jungle in front of him. Someone yelled, "We're going into the trees," and as the helicopter smashed into the jungle, Tyme realized the voice hadn't been panicked. It had been warning him so that he could prepare himself for the coming crash.

SANTINI WAITED OUTSIDE the interrogation room while the Vietnamese soldier continued to question the woman. He had listened for a few minutes, but had felt himself sickened by the whole process, so he had left the map room, telling the sergeant there that he would wait in the corridor.

Pacing up and down, he picked at the thick rough planks that formed the wall. He kicked at its base and studied the wood, making pictures out of the grain. Once or twice he put an ear against the door, but heard nothing.

Finally the door opened. The Vietnamese soldier who had interrogated the woman left without a glance toward Santini. The prisoner, trailed by an MP came next. She wore a rough tan cotton shirt stained with blood, and her hands were still bound behind her.

"Where are you taking her?" Santini asked the MP.

The MP reached out and put a hand on his prisoner's shoulder, stopping her. "First I'm taking her over to the provost marshal and then we'll probably take her to the POW compound."

Santini looked into the Vietnamese woman's eyes, wondering if there was something smoldering there. He could see pain in them, but he didn't think there was hate. The enemy expected rough treatment, but if it was tempered with kindness, if he demonstrated that the Americans weren't as brutal as their Vietnamese counterparts, he could make an ally.

"Why don't you swing by the hospital first?" Santini asked.

The MP shrugged. "Why?"

"Use your head, man. She's just a girl and may not have known what she was doing."

"Hey. A zip is just a zip."

Santini shook his head and stared at the man. He was young, probably no more than nineteen or twenty, like so many of the soldiers being sent to Vietnam. The Army took them in, sent them to a school to get them an MOS and then shipped them immediately to Vietnam. No training was given to them about the people of Vietnam. No thought was given to the fact that the locals were human beings. There were no indoctrination courses suggesting the Vietcong and the North Vietnamese were less than human, but there was nothing to stop that belief from developing.

The Vietnamese soldier returned, looked at the three people and shook his head. He mumbled something and then spun around, heading for the door again. It was as if he no longer cared what happened to the woman now that she had given him all the information she had.

Santini moved forward and touched the woman on the shoulder. She looked up at him, tears in her eyes. He could see fear in there now.

"Okay, Sergeant, here's the deal," said Santini. "I have a jeep outside. You and I and the young woman are going to get in it and we're going to drive her over to the hospital and let them treat her."

"I'm not sure we're allowed to do that."

"Consider it an order. I'll go with you. Then we'll take her to the POW compound or over to the military prison. Or maybe we'll take her over to the Fifth SF Headquarters so that a couple of our people can talk to her."

"I don't know."

"I'll have Major Madden call the provost marshal and clear it. You won't catch any flak."

"Hey, Santini," came a voice from inside, "you want a briefing or not?"

"Can it wait for a couple of hours?"

"Okay."

"Then I'll come back." He pulled the MP away from the door and shut it. As they moved down the corridor, Santini asked, "How much do you weigh, Sergeant?"

The MP shrugged. "About one-ninety, I guess."

"And you're what. Six-one? Six-two?"

"Just over six-two. Why?"

"Well, I noticed that you're armed with a .45 and a nightstick. You tower over the lady. She seems to be tame enough. Is it necessary to keep her hands tied?"

"SOP. You can't trust these zips. She could pull a knife or something."

They reached the stairway leading up out of the bunker. Santini stopped and said, "I watched you in the interrogation room. It was obvious to me that she wasn't armed. I think that between the two of us we could take her in a fair fight, and if she makes a run for it, I doubt she'll get far. You can gun her down if she runs. So why don't you untie her?"

"Look Sergeant," said the MP, "you're not in my chain of command. I have rules and regulations I have to obey. One of them is that the prisoner is to be restrained during transportation.''

''True,'' said Santini, ''but I still outrank you by two stripes and I would like you to untie the prisoner. If she escapes, it'll be my fault.''

The MP stood for a moment, staring at Santini. Then he shrugged. ''If you want to be nice to the zips, I guess it's no skin off my nose.'' He spun the woman around and fumbled at the knots on the rope.

''And, Sergeant, let's try to remember that these are people, too. They may be the enemy and they may not like us, but they are people.''

''Yeah,'' he grumbled. ''I've seen what these people do to the Americans they capture.''

Santini wanted to respond to that. He wanted to tell the MP that it made no sense for them to come down to the level of the VC or NVA. No matter what anyone said, the enemy was human. In battle you were supposed to kill or capture them. But once the battle was over, you weren't supposed to move among the wounded and cut their throats. A soldier could be ruthless in battle, he could kill a sentry or an enemy to gain the objective, which ultimately was the winning of the war, but he didn't have to become an animal to do it.

Instead, he said, ''Thank you, Sergeant.'' He took the woman's elbow and guided her up the steps. She stared at him, but he thought some of the fear had left her.

The MPs at the gate looked troubled when they appeared, but said nothing as Santini signed out. They watched Santini help the woman into the jeep and the MP climb into the rear. Santini started the engine and turned down the road so that he could get them over to the Eighth Field Hospital.

They were stopped at the door and held there by an orderly who didn't want the Vietnamese woman inside, but then one of the nurses saw what was happening and rushed over.

''What's going on?'' she demanded.

Santini liked her immediately. She was a small woman, barely larger than the Vietnamese girl, with short black hair and a thin face. There were dark circles under her eyes, and she blinked rapidly, as if she had just left a dark theater for the bright light of the afternoon sun.

"Your man won't let us in," said Santini. "I wanted someone to take care of the woman."

The nurse saw that the prisoner had been beaten. "This is your handiwork?" she asked Santini, anger in her voice.

"No, ma'am, I'm just trying to correct a bad situation, is all."

The nurse put an arm lightly around the girl's shoulders. "You come with me." When both Santini and the MP started to follow, she ordered, "You wait out here."

As the MP started forward again, Santini put a restraining hand on him. "You wait." To the nurse he said, "I need to come with you because she's VC, but I won't get in the way."

The nurse stopped and looked over her shoulder at Santini. It looked as if she was going to deny him permission, but then she nodded curtly. "Okay. You can come along, but the other one has to wait out here."

"It's all right, Sergeant," Santini said. "I won't let the prisoner escape. You just relax."

"But—"

"You wait," said Santini. "I'll keep an eye on her." With that Santini vanished down the hall with the nurse and the Vietnamese girl.

4

DUC HOA

After a quick lunch in the team house, Gerber and Fetterman followed Sergeant Albright across the compound. There wasn't much to see. Red dust clung to everything. A short tower, with a ladder leading up into it, was surrounded by a wall of sandbags, and open swamp stretched as far as they could see to the south, where the Song Vam Co Dong wound its way toward the South China Sea.

Albright climbed into the jeep. "It isn't much, but it's the best we have." He turned in the driver's seat and leaned to the rear so that he could flip on the PRC-25. "SOP is for us to have the radio on all the time we're off the compound."

Fetterman got into the rear and studied the radio while Gerber took the passenger's seat. Albright turned the ignition switch and the engine caught, died and caught again. It rumbled for a moment, seemed about to die, belched a cloud of black smoke and then started running smoothly.

"Yeah," said Albright, "I know what you're thinking, but once it gets warmed up, it works just fine."

"If it breaks down, can you fix it?" asked Gerber.

"No, sir. I just call in on the radio and someone comes out to take a look. It's really no big deal."

Fetterman touched Gerber on the shoulder. "Don't worry, sir. If the jeep breaks, I think I can fix it."

"We can head to the south or to the north and west," said Albright, leaning an elbow on top of the steering wheel.

Without a word, Fetterman handed a map up to Gerber. The captain took the map, opened it and refolded it until Duc Hoa was in the center. He saw that there were plantations scattered throughout the area, a dozen or more canals, swamp and numerous villages, some of them so small they weren't even located on the map. There was a general area for them.

"Let's head north toward Bao Trai."

"Yeah," said Albright. "That road is fairly good and the enemy hasn't mined it."

"You sweep it often?"

Albright shot a glance over his shoulder. "Don't have to. Farmers use it. They keep it clean. If they don't dig up the mines to get rid of them, they step on them and explode them."

"Wonderful system," said Fetterman.

Albright dropped the jeep into gear, spun the wheel and took off in a cloud of red dust and flying dirt as he popped the clutch. He slid around a corner, throwing up dirt, and jammed on the brakes, sliding to a halt near the gate. Two Vietnamese strikers wearing OD shorts and a bandolier of ammo ran from their bunker to open up.

The jeep roared through the gate, and Albright turned onto a dirt road that was a red scar through the plush green countryside. Gerber put a hand to his eyes to shield them and then wiped the sweat from his forehead. He dug into his pocket and took out his sunglasses. Normally he didn't wear them because he didn't want to get too used to them, but the sun reflecting from the water of the swamps and the canals made it almost impossible to see. He turned and saw that Fetterman seemed not to be bothered by the brightness.

Gerber stared at the people in the fields. There were the normal number of old men and old women, dressed in black pants and rough cotton shirts. Nearly everyone wore a coolie hat for protection from the sun.

Fetterman tapped Gerber on the shoulder. "Awful lot of people of military age in the fields."

Gerber nodded but didn't say anything. He had noticed it, too—young men who would normally be hiding during the heat of the day if only to keep out of the way of the South Vietnamese military and the American Army. Now they were in the fields wearing black shorts and no shirts. They didn't look down when the jeep passed but returned the stares of the occupants.

They came to a group of three young men walking on the side of the road. Unlike the peasants, they didn't leap into the ditch but stayed where they were, glaring. Gerber met their gazes and felt the hatred behind the eyes. As they drove by, Gerber turned in the seat, keeping his eyes on them.

"You think we should check their IDs?" asked Fetterman.

"Wouldn't do any good," said Gerber. Then he reached out and tapped Albright on the shoulder. "Stop the jeep!"

Albright jammed on the brakes, and they slid to a halt. Gerber got out, his weapon in his hand. He didn't have to call to the men because they hadn't moved. Gerber felt Fetterman's presence beside him and asked, "You notice anything about those guys?"

"You mean like they're all military age, they don't look like farmers and they all have muscled shoulders suggesting that they carry backpacks?"

"Yes, and that big guy is wearing an NVA haircut." Gerber slipped off the safety on his M-16. He glanced over his shoulder and saw that Albright was standing behind the jeep, his weapon cradled in his arms.

Fetterman advanced on the men and said in Vietnamese, "I would like to see your ID."

They looked at one another, pretending they didn't understand. Fetterman stood like a thin, smiling Buddha, waiting. He stared at the man in the center, eyes locked on those of the young man, who finally dropped his gaze and reached to the rear. Fetterman tensed, but the man produced a laminated government issue ID card.

Fetterman took it, held it up so that Gerber could see it and then handed it back. He bowed slightly and thanked the man, wishing him a safe journey. With that Fetterman turned and headed back to the jeep.

"I knew it," said Gerber. "NVA."

"Yeah," agreed Fetterman. "That ID is a dead giveaway. I'll bet if we asked one of the farmers for his ID he either wouldn't have it or it would be a worn, tattered document."

"You two satisfied?" asked Albright.

"Well, those guys answered one question," said Gerber. He waited until Albright had the jeep heading down the road again and said, "Are there a lot of men like that around here?"

"More than normal and more showing up all the time."

Gerber turned and looked at Fetterman. "You seen enough, Tony?"

"Let's check out the marketplace before we head back."

"Sergeant," said Gerber.

"Couple of miles more."

They entered a small town of mud hootches with rusted tin roofs. There were bright signs on some of them and mud fences that separated the doors from the roadways. One building had a dilapidated porch. Two young Vietnamese girls sat in the shade and were surrounded by young men. Gerber tried not to stare, taking in as much detail as possible as they drove by. Again he noticed that men stared rather than looked away and that they all had short hair with white sidewalls. More NVA trying to blend into the countryside.

They came to a long, low building with a thatched roof and only a few walls that separated the stalls from one another. At one end there were seven or eight fifty-five-gallon drums, wooden crates, tin cans and the remains of C-ration boxes. Tied to a pole near them were two pigs. A boy sat nearby, watching them and ignoring everything else.

Gerber could see that there was food stacked in some of the stalls. Meat was hanging from the roof, some of it seeming to move as the flies crawled on it. A group of people, mostly young women, sat talking to one another.

"Looks kind of dead."

Albright pulled to the side and stopped. "Normally this place is jumping. You can get anything you want here. I mean everything." He pointed to the women. "They're available most of the time, but now, who knows? Couple of guys from the Twenty-fifth said the women now claim to be hostesses. No longer are they whores."

Gerber put a foot up on the dashboard. For a moment he wished he smoked. He wiped a hand across his forehead, then on the front of his fatigue jacket, leaving a ragged sweat stain.

"Tony, you seen enough now?"

"I've seen plenty, Captain. There has to be three times the normal number of military-age men around here."

"Then we know that something is happening," said Gerber. He didn't need to explain that a buildup of enemy forces meant that something was coming.

"I guess we can head on back."

"That is," added Fetterman, "if you're sure the same thing is repeated all over the area."

Albright nodded. "It's the same. One day there are barely enough military-age males around to do the work and the next there are twice as many. No signs of weapons or military equipment, but you can bet that if we ran a search-and-destroy we'd find a lot of it."

"Why don't you?"

"Orders from Saigon. They don't want us making waves now. Contact is down, casualties are down and no one wants to stir the pot."

"Yeah," said Gerber. "I've heard all that before."

Albright turned in the seat so that he could back up. He worked the stick, grinding the gears. As he pulled out onto the road, there was a pop from the radio in the back, a burst of static and a garbled message.

"What's your call sign?" asked Fetterman.

"Warlord Seven."

Fetterman picked up the handset and squeezed the button. "Say again for Warlord Seven."

"Roger, Seven. We've lost contact with Warlord Two. He was traveling in your vicinity."

"Wait one," said Fetterman. He moved the handset from his ear and leaned forward. "You have any idea where Two was going?"

"He said he'd be heading toward Bao Trai and then over to Ap Tan Hoa. That's a village complex out near Hiep Hoa and west of Duc Hue."

"You want to swing up in that direction," said Gerber, "feel free to do so. It'll just give us all the opportunity to take a longer look at the AO."

"Sounds good, sir."

Fetterman raised the handset. "Warlord Base, this is Seven. We'll swing through the Alpha Oscar and see what we can scare up."

"Roger, Seven. Be advised that Six wants a report every thirty minutes on your progress."

"Roger that." Fetterman dropped the handset back onto the seat and asked, "This unusual?"

"Nah. Two is always running off on his own and forgets to check in so that we have to go looking for him," commented Gerber.

"Seems pretty slack," commented Gerber.

"Well, sir, you know how it is. Can't always make radio check when you're supposed to so that everyone gets his balls in an uproar. You can't blow it off because it might be the one time the guy needs help."

"I'm not complaining," said Gerber. "I'm merely pointing out that your Six lets you run around with a little more freedom than I would."

"Yes, sir."

They approached a hamlet from the southeast. This was another of the mud-and-thatch villages. There was a network of roadways that were little more than tracks of bare ground full of potholes and stagnant water. Paint had been splashed on some of the buildings in an attempt to make them more presentable. Signs in both Vietnamese and English marked the two bars that stood opposite each other. On the porch of one, at a small round table, sat three Vietnamese girls. They didn't look up as the jeep approached.

Albright turned toward the bar and stopped. He shut off the engine. "You wait here and I'll find out if they've seen anything."

"I take it you can speak Vietnamese," said Fetterman.

"Some. But the girls can speak some English. I'll be able to talk to them."

Fetterman shrugged. "Suit yourself."

As Albright got out of the jeep, taking his weapon with him, Gerber closed his eyes and let the silence wash over him. Far from Saigon and the American fire support bases scattered around Highway One, there was little sound except for a birdcall in the distance or a shout and the discordant music of the Vietnamese from a radio the girls had.

Gerber opened his eyes and watched one of the girls stand. She was short, under five feet tall, but slim and perfectly proportioned so that it was impossible to tell a thing about her until Albright approached. Then it was obvious that she was tiny. She wore black pajamas that hid her shape but not her long, silky hair. She grabbed Albright's free arm, pressing herself to him, her voice cool and seductive.

The other girls sat quietly, waiting for either Fetterman or Gerber to make a move but unwilling to start it themselves. They stayed where they were, neither smiling nor waving.

Albright sat in the free chair. One of the girls got up and ran inside, returning with a Coke bottle made from clear glass. She set it and a glass with a single, large chunk of ice in front of Albright. He poured the Coke in, let it fizz for a moment and then took a drink. With the ritual complete, he began talking rapidly, his hands waving animatedly.

After a few minutes Albright drained his Coke and stood. He bent over and kissed the tiny girl on the forehead and then made his way back to the jeep. Putting his weapon between the seats, he climbed in.

"They said one of our jeeps came through about two hours ago. They didn't pay much attention because the man driving didn't slow down. I think it was Thompson."

"You know," said Fetterman, "you could have brought us each a Coke."

Albright shrugged. "You could have bought your own." He started the engine and fought it into reverse. He backed out and started off again.

As they drove through the village, Gerber took off his hat and wiped the sweat from his face. The wind from the motion of the jeep cooled him slightly.

They left the village and turned onto a road that was little more than a track across the high ground. High weeds grew in the center, and there was water from the swamp on both sides. Right and left was a sea of grass and reeds, broken occasionally by clumps of trees or high, dry ground.

Far in front of them, a mile or more, was another of the small villages. Hootches with flashing tin roofs were hidden in a clump of trees.

"That's Ap Tan Hoa Four," said Albright. "It's a hotbed of Communist activity."

"Meaning?"

"Just that if there is a Communist cadre in the area, they live there. They maintain a low profile and cause trouble once in a great while. I don't think there's a lot of support for them in the villages."

They came close and slowed down. Finally Albright stopped the jeep and sat staring at the village for a moment. There was nothing to see, just the hootches, none of which were painted like those of the last ville. No signs and no people. The fields around it were deserted.

"I don't like this," said Fetterman.

Albright didn't turn to look. He just said, "I don't like this, either. Something's wrong."

BROMHEAD WAS SWEATING in the midafternoon sun, wondering if he shouldn't delegate this job. He couldn't remember Gerber ever helping to string barbed wire, but then, he did remember his former captain filling sandbags and stacking them. He also recalled Gerber helping to rebuild the team house and working under a jeep. It wasn't that Gerber refused to help string barbed wire, he just never had the opportunity.

Bromhead wiped the sweat from his face, then looked toward the sun, wishing there were a few clouds in the sky or that a rainstorm was brewing. Anything to break the heat.

As he bent to continue staking down one end of the wire, he wondered if it did any good. He had seen a demonstration put on by a former VC sapper. The man had shown how easy it was to penetrate the concertina around the American bases. He had moved through the thickest of it as if there was no barrier. He didn't even rattle the beer cans that were hung all over the place. When he finished, he had pointed to ways to make the wire more effective, telling his audience that the wires around the camps were little more than ways to slightly slow an attack. Sappers could get through them quickly and silently.

Bromhead had asked if they should just forget about the wire and the man had said no, that the wire was important. It meant that the enemy had to plan their attack with it in mind. A large-scale assault meant the enemy had to send in the sappers to blow holes in the wire and that gave the defenders some warning about the attack.

Given that, Bromhead tried to hide the trip flares and mines he was putting in so that the sapper wouldn't see them as he tried to work his way through the wire.

He stood when he heard a shout behind him and turned to see Mildebrandt hurrying toward him. While he waited, he mopped his face with his sleeve, soaking it.

Mildebrandt halted and gulped air. "Got a radio call from Hornet Operations in Cu Chi. Wanted to know if their aircraft had been here or not."

"And you told them it had been."

"Yes, sir, sure did. They asked for the takeoff time and their destination. I told them we thought it was heading for Tay Ninh. And I found out that it apparently never got there. They were backtracking, to see if they could locate it. They wanted to know if the pilot had reported any trouble to us."

Bromhead looked at the ground and kicked at the small box. "Shit."

"I figured we'd get a couple of squads into the field—"

"And do what?" asked Bromhead. "You know what those things cruise at. A hundred miles an hour. They took off a couple of hours ago. They could be hundreds of miles from here. Where do you plan to look?"

"Tyme's on that chopper."

Bromhead felt a cold hand on his stomach. He stared at Mildebrandt. "I know that Sergeant Tyme was on the aircraft, but I'd like to know what in hell I'm supposed to do about it."

"Captain, we've got to do something."

Bromhead was going to respond and then thought about it. There was almost no chance that a ground patrol would be able to locate the chopper if it had gone down in the jungles around Song Be. If something had happened and they had managed to get to one of the American camps, then Tyme would be calling in. But he knew that he had to do something, even if it was only a token gesture.

Bromhead touched his lips with the back of his hand. "Okay. First we'd better see if we can get any airlift support. Then I'll want a couple of patrols ready to go. If we overfly their route we might spot them. If not, then we'll go in on the ground."

"Yes, sir," said Mildebrandt. "I'll take one, and Sergeant Bocker said he wanted to take the other."

Bromhead picked up the cardboard carton, then looked at the sun again. "It's going to be close to dark before we can get anyone into the field. Maybe we'd better wait until first light."

Mildebrandt nodded. "Militarily it makes sense to wait until morning."

Bromhead wrapped an arm around the cardboard box and held up his hand. "I know what you're thinking, and you're probably right. It's just that I don't want to sacrifice a couple more men in a gesture. Between you and me, you know that anything we do isn't going to help all that much. There really isn't much we can do without aviation support."

"So we give it up," said Mildebrandt.

"No. But we don't run off in fourteen different directions, either."

They reached the gate, and two Vietnamese strikers came toward them. Bromhead handed over the box and turned toward the commo bunker.

As they entered, Bocker said, "Captain, I've talked with the CO of the Hornets and the battalion commander down there. Hornet Six said he'd give us anything we needed and said that a couple of choppers would be here in thirty minutes. We could deploy them as we saw fit. Black Baron Six, the battalion CO, said he was pulling in aircraft from the Crusaders, too. Have them begin a search starting in Tay Ninh."

Bromhead moved to a map that was mounted on the wall. He looked at Song Be and then Tay Ninh. "That's an awful lot of territory we have to search. An awful lot."

5

DOWNTOWN SAIGON

Le Tran took the happy Marines through the wide streets with their heavy traffic of jeeps, trucks and Lambrettas. She led them past honky-tonk bars that wailed with country and western music, around more bars that blasted rock and through crowds of prostitutes who tried to steal the Marines with offers of everything the Marines could imagine. Finally Le Tran was tired of the challenges and yelled for a taxi. It swerved across several lanes of traffic, amid squealing tires and blaring horns, and screeched to a halt inches from them.

It was a car of indeterminate color and origin. It might have once been a Ford, or it might have been a Chevy, but so many parts had been replaced in such a mixture that it was impossible to tell. They squeezed into the back seat, Le Tran sitting on Lockridge's lap, wiggling her bottom as if to get comfortable. Lockridge felt himself respond with an ache that spread from his groin to his stomach.

As they roared through the traffic, Lockridge lost track of the route. He occasionally saw the wide streets lined with beautiful buildings give way to mud tracks that were lined with ramshackle hootches cobbled together with plywood and cardboard stolen from the American bases. Some of them had tin roofs but many did not. Wires ran from poles into the structures to provide some kind of electrical power. An odor of stagnant water, dead fish and feces drifted on a hot breeze that rattled the buildings.

They came to an area that wasn't quite as run-down, the hootches built from stone and brick. The taxi drew to a halt on a street with disintegrating pavement after Le Tran told the driver to pull over. She scrambled from the back seat, managed to press her breast against Lockridge and gave him a view of her legs all the way to the crotch.

She stood next to the driver's door and whispered, "Please pay him."

Lockridge pulled the MPC from his pocket and listened as the driver told him the ride would cost one thousand piasters. Lockridge didn't care. He threw the money at the driver and followed Le Tran as she walked up the broken sidewalk to the front door. As she opened it, she stopped and smiled. "Well, come on."

Lockridge looked at Jones and then nearly ran up the sidewalk. Jones moved slower, as if worried about a trap of some kind, but both entered the house. Like the exterior, it was run-down. The tiled floor of the entryway was dirty and scarred. The walls needed paint, and there was a musty smell in the air. To the right was a large room with old furniture. Lockridge entered and noticed that the house had once been expensive. There were hardwood floors and decorative carvings on the wood trim of the walls. A huge window dominated one side, but part of it was covered with plywood.

"You be seated," said Le Tran, "and I will go talk to my sister."

As Le Tran left the room, Lockridge turned slowly. There was an American record player in one corner with a selection of albums from the PX. Several small tables were scattered about, but only two held lamps. Lockridge sat on the couch and felt the springs against his back.

"What do you think?" he asked.

Jones stepped to the window and looked out. "They had money once, I think. But Christ, Jim, no one knows where we are. Hell, I don't know where I am."

"You afraid of Le Tran?"

"No, but I don't like this. We're not even armed. We started out for the little café across from the embassy and now who knows where the fuck we are?"

"Jesus, will you relax? We've fallen into a deal here, and you want to ignore it because you're afraid of a girl?"

Jones turned from the window and leaned against the wall. "I'm not afraid of the girl."

At that moment, Le Tran returned leading another young woman who held one hand in front of her face and who was looking at the floor.

"My sister is very shy. She does not speak good English like me and she does not meet many soldiers."

Lockridge got to his feet. "Please tell her that we're more than happy to meet her."

The sister stepped out, dropped her hand and smiled. She looked more like a European than she did a Vietnamese. She had a narrow face, a long, slender nose and almost round eyes. They weren't dark, but a washed-out gray. She was wearing a pink *ao dai* over black pajama bottoms.

"I glad to meet you all," she said. Her voice was soft, almost impossible to hear, and although her words were right, she seemed to have no accent.

Jones stepped forward, his mouth open. He held out a hand. "I'm very happy to meet you, too."

The woman looked at him, smiled broadly and then dropped her eyes. She didn't take his hand, but moved closer to him.

Lockridge clapped his hands. "Now, Le Tran, if everyone's ready, I thought we'd go find something to eat."

"Oh, before we go, my sister, Tri Tran, would like to change clothes, if you do not mind."

"Mind," said Jones. "Hell, I'll help her if she'd like."

Tri Tran giggled, shook her head and fled from the room. Le Tran said, "If you will excuse me, I shall go help her make the proper selection."

When the women were gone, Lockridge said, "Do you still want to complain about this?"

"No," said Jones, shaking his head. "Not at all. I think you were right." He moved closer and lowered his voice. "This is great. Did you see her? She's a beauty."

"And she seems to like you," said Lockridge.

"Yeah, I noticed that."

"So here's the plan. We've got to separate them. Then I can head back here with Le Tran while you keep Tri Tran out. Give me an hour or so after we disappear and then you can come back here. But I'll need an hour."

"How come you get to come back here?"

"Because I started this, and it's only fair that I reap the first rewards."

With that decided, they both sat down to wait for the thrills that they knew would come.

ROBIN MORROW SAT in the city room, her feet propped on her desk as she stared out the window. She couldn't see anything except a patch of blue sky and the plain white front of the building across the street. She leaned to the right, opened a drawer and pulled out a handkerchief. Wiping her face with it, she looked at the smear of sweat, then tossed it aside.

Mark Hodges left his cubicle and walked toward her. He smiled broadly as he approached and then waved. His eyes studied the curves of her bare legs. He approved of the cutoff jumpsuits she wore.

"You get anything at that briefing?" he asked.

Morrow leaned the other way, pawed through her camera bag and came up with a notebook. She flipped through it and found the beginning of her notes on the briefing. "It was one of those nonbriefing briefings. A little activity around the area and a suggestion of more to come."

"Sounds like a load of crap."

"Yeah, well," said Morrow, "I got the impression that the guy was talking around something. He kept coming back to these small incidents. A mortar attack here and an ambush there. Couple of people kept coming back to the fact that nothing major is going on."

Hodges scratched his knee. "That's just these military boys trying to justify their existence. If there's no war, then they all go back to the States and the promotions and opportunities slow down."

"I don't know about that," countered Morrow. "There seems to be something in the air."

"That's the humidity," said Hodges. "Or dead fish. Listen, this thing's about over. The writing is on the wall. With nothing happening, the war can be turned over to the South Vietnamese."

Morrow dropped her feet to the floor. "You know, Mark, you keep saying that. Everyone keeps saying that, but the military seems to be waiting for something."

"Politics pure and simple. These guys are trying to justify their jobs, just as I said."

Morrow shook her head. "I don't know about that. I can feel something."

"Okay, you're such a hotshot photojournalist, you tell me what's going on. What does your Green Beret captain have to say about this?"

Morrow smiled. "I haven't been able to reach him today. He's in the field."

"Probably looking for the enemy that you think is running all over the place."

"There was something—"

"Robin, I'll let you in on a little secret." Hodges looked around as if afraid there were spies in the newsroom. "I received a message from home suggesting we think about cutting the staff here. With the winding down of the war, too much effort is being expended. That's the general feeling at home."

"I think everyone is overlooking something. That Major Hobbs who briefed us refused to say outright that the war was almost over. He seemed to know something we didn't and was trying not to deceive us."

Hodges stood and raised his hands as if surrendering. "I'll tell you what. You think that something is coming, you put it in the form of a memo to me and I'll forward it, but I'll tell you right now that you're going to look like a jerk."

"Thanks for the encouragement," said Morrow.

"Robin, don't take it the wrong way, but this is your first war. You haven't seen them end, and I tell you, all the signs are there. The enemy's in disarray. He's making harassment raids to improve the terms of surrender, but there's nothing he can do. He's shot his wad. It's all over but for the shouting and the parades."

Morrow nodded slowly, as if listening carefully, but in the back of her mind she remembered reading about the Battle of the Bulge. The German army had been all but defeated. It had been in disarray and retreating on all fronts. Then, suddenly, an army that no one had known about had appeared and everyone was caught by surprise. For some reason Morrow believed that history was about to repeat itself.

SANTINI SAT in Major Madden's office, concentrating on the Vietnamese girl as she ate the sandwich that Santini had gotten for her. She didn't speak and didn't look up. She just concentrated on the meal.

Madden studied her for a moment, then turned toward Santini. "What in hell did you bring her here for?"

Santini shrugged. "What was I supposed to do, Major? I told you what the Vietnamese were doing."

Madden straightened the papers on his desk, tapped the ends together so that they were neat and then set the whole mess into his out basket. He looked at the girl again and saw the faint stains from her blood. "I don't know. I can tell you that it's a domestic problem, one that we shouldn't get involved in."

"Right," said Santini. "Just let the Vietnamese murder one another because they're Vietnamese."

"Knock it off, Sergeant," snapped Madden. "You know what I mean. This is something the Vietnamese should handle internally, without interference from us. You're just making problems, and in the end we'll be told that it's none of our business."

"Granted, Major. But I just couldn't allow those animals to get their hands on her. We have the opportunity to create an ally."

"Our job isn't to create allies."

Santini remembered the new policy of winning the hearts and minds of the Vietnamese people, a policy designed to create allies, but he knew better than to say anything about it to Madden.

The girl wadded up the paper and held it in her hand. She looked from one man to the other. "I go now?"

"You didn't tell me she could speak English," said Madden.

"Hell, Major, I didn't know."

"I go now?" she asked again.

Santini moved from the couch and crouched before her. He looked up into her eyes. "I'm afraid we can't let you go right now."

"But I help you. I give you . . . give you . . . help and you let me go."

"What's your name?" asked Santini.

"I am Co."

"Well, Co, I'm afraid you made a mistake by bringing the explosives onto the base."

She shook her head. "But I did not know about the explosives. A man gave me the case to carry. It is my first day. I do not understand."

Santini shot a look at Madden. "Major?"

He held up his hands. "She was caught bringing the explosives in. It's an open-and-shut case and there isn't much we can do about it."

"But we could move her over to one of our compounds, tell the men there the story and have them keep an eye on her."

The woman seized on that. "Yes. I do that. I work for you now."

"Sergeant . . ." said Madden.

"I know secret," said Co. "I do not tell. I keep secret because Vietnamese hurt me. I tell you."

"All right, Co," said Santini. "What do you know?"

"The Vietcong will attack your base. They come for Tet and destroy all around here. They say that base going to be gone after Tet. All Americans will be dead."

Madden stood and moved to the front of his desk. "That's very interesting, but if you know nothing of the enemy and the explosives you carried in, how do you know that an attack is coming?"

"I hear them talk. I not stupid. I listen, but I do not talk. They do not think I understand them."

Now Santini turned on Madden. "Well, Major?"

"I'll call and see what I can arrange."

"You'll have to call the provost marshal and coordinate with him, too. Let him know that we'll take responsibility for the prisoner. While you're doing that, I can see about finding a place for Co."

"Great, Sergeant. I'm real happy that you've got us involved in this."

6

OUTSIDE AP TAN HOA
FOUR

"I'm not sure that driving through the village is such a hot idea," said Gerber.

"Neither am I," responded Albright.

Gerber climbed out of the jeep, then checked the safety on his weapon. Fetterman jumped over the side and stood behind him.

"Okay, Sergeant," said Gerber, "why don't you ease through the ville and we'll follow you?"

"I don't know."

"If you move slow enough, we'll be there to lend support if you need it. I just don't want us all grouped together until we get back into the open."

Albright nodded as he reached over and picked up his M-16. He slipped off the safety and set the weapon on the passenger's seat. Finally he felt ready and slipped the jeep into gear. He let out the clutch slowly; the engine coughed once then caught.

Fetterman hurried to the other side of the track, his M-3 grease gun in his hands. He started after the jeep, his head swiveling slowly from side to side as he scanned the ground around him for the enemy.

Open fields surrounded the village of Ap Tan Hoa Four. There were swamps and rice paddies with only a couple of clumps of trees visible more than half a klick away. The road curved through the village so that the scattered hootches hid what was around the bend.

And still there were no people. It was as if they had hidden from the heat of the afternoon, although Gerber knew that the Vietnamese didn't have a tradition of siestas. They worked in their rice paddies throughout the afternoon because nearly everyone was afraid to be out when darkness fell. After sundown, the soldiers came out and shot at everything that moved. If the farmer had to get something done, he did it during the day.

Gerber entered the ville. The first structure, a mud hootch with a thatched roof, sat to his right, set back from the road. A mud fence reinforced with woven branches surrounded part of it. On one side was a family bunker and on the other was the pen for the water buffalo.

As he passed the hootch, he tried to see into the interior, but couldn't. He listened closely, but there was no sound. The village was deathly quiet. The only noise was the idling of the jeep's engine as Albright waited for Gerber and Fetterman to close the gap.

They rounded the bend and now the open fields on the west side of the village were visible. Standing on a wide portion of the road was another jeep, sitting low on one side as if it had a flat tire. Albright stopped his jeep, and Gerber caught up to him. There was no sign of the missing man.

"Approach it slowly," cautioned Gerber.

"Yes, sir."

Gerber glanced at Fetterman. The master sergeant nodded and began moving forward slowly. Gerber wiped the sweat from his forehead with his shoulder, leaving a wet, ragged stain. His heart began to race, the blood pounding in his ears. There wasn't much that could cause someone to desert his jeep without radioing in.

Then, as he got closer, he noticed what seemed to be a shape partially hidden by a rice paddy dike. The object looked like a misshapen head without a hat, and part of a shoulder. The top of the dike appeared wet, and Gerber was suddenly sure that he could hear flies buzzing over the sound of the jeep's engine.

Fetterman leaped from the track to the wetness of the rice paddy opposite them, his eyes moving, searching. Albright slowed the jeep for a moment, staring at the ground near his vehicle. Slowly he reached for his weapon and got out of the jeep. He walked around the front and slipped in the mud on the side of the dike. He regained his balance quickly and stood upright.

Gerber approached carefully. The others had found a body. Albright turned to Gerber. "It's Sergeant Thompson. But his face is all wrong."

Gerber shot a glance at Fetterman to make certain the master sergeant had them covered. Satisfied he moved forward and dropped into the paddy. He rolled the body over and saw the problem. Thompson's face was distorted because of the pressure created by a shot to the back of the head.

Gerber's gaze drifted to the immediate surroundings. The ground around the front of the jeep was littered with empty brass casings. The forward section of the vehicle was riddled with bullet holes, and a couple of empty magazines lay under the jeep. Gerber looked at the rear section, but there was no radio.

The captain swallowed, his thoughts racing. It was obvious. Thompson had been ambushed on the open road. He had held the enemy off until he'd run out of ammo and then they had captured him. The bloodstain on the grass at the side of the road showed that he had been shot there before his body was dumped into the rice paddy.

Gerber checked the corpse and found the bullet hole in the back of the head. There was a tattoo effect around it, which suggested that the barrel of the weapon had been only inches from Thompson's head. He had been executed.

"Okay," said Gerber. "We've got to get out of here." He reached out and grabbed Thompson's shoulder, dragging him from the water. Although his weapons and his knife were missing, he still wore his webgear.

"Tony, they can't be far away."

"Probably holed up in the ville."

Gerber stood and surveyed the village. Still there was no movement. Everyone was in hiding. Now it made sense. With a dead American lying in the field, none of them wanted to be seen. It would give the Americans an excellent opportunity to shoot a few of them to get even.

"Captain," said Fetterman. "Movement to the right, at the edge of the ville."

Gerber eased closer to Fetterman and dropped to the little cover provided by the short dikes that surrounded the rice paddies.

Without pointing, Fetterman said, "See that large palm with all the dead leaves? Now look to the right about ten, twelve meters and there's a rusting oil drum."

"Got it."

"I saw a flash behind that. Nothing more now."

Gerber stared at the open area. All he saw was flat, dry ground covered with red dust. But there was no sign of movement. A gentle breeze stirred the dead branches of the palm, but it did nothing to relieve the heat. Gerber was suddenly aware of the heat and humidity. Sweat was running down his temples and dripping off the end of his nose. He stuck his bottom lip out and blew the droplets away. He could also feel the moisture trickling down his sides and back.

He was about to tell Fetterman to keep watching, when he saw movement. A streak of khaki dived from the doorway of a hootch to the protection of the rusted oil drum. "Albright," he whispered, "get ready. They're coming for us."

Albright scrambled from behind the dike and rolled to his stomach near the front of Thompson's jeep. Keeping the muzzle of his M-16 out of the dirt, he crawled along the side of the vehicle until he reached his own. He got to his knees near the front tire and looked over the hood at the village. Now it was completely quiet. No barking dogs, no calling birds, no bellowing water buffalo. It was as if all the civilians, knowing that a fight was coming, had fled, taking their animals with them.

Albright slipped to his left and then leaned over the passenger's seat, reaching for the radio mounted in the back. He pulled the handset toward him, stretched it out and flipped it on. An idea suddenly hit him. The enemy had gotten to Thompson's radio. Unless he had zeroed the radio, had twisted all the dials for the frequency to zeros, the enemy now had their company frequency. Albright made his first call.

At Duc Hoa the commo sergeant answered Albright's whispered message.

As soon as he got the acknowledgment, Albright said, "Primary has been compromised. Go to secondary."

"Roger."

Albright leaned in again and changed the frequency. Once the tuning squeal faded, he slipped out of the jeep and leaned against the rear tire. He made another call.

When it was rogered, he said, "Be advised that we have located Warlord Two as KIA near Alpha Tango Hotel Four."

There was hesitation at the other end, and Albright knew that the information about Thompson's death was being passed around. Then came, "You are to return ASAP."

"Roger. Be advised that we have possible enemy contact on the sierra side of Alpha Tango Hotel."

"Do you require arty support?"

"That's a negative at this time."

"Roger. Keep us informed."

Albright rogered and was tempted to toss the handset back into the jeep but then thought better of it. He turned, getting to his knees so that he could see over the rear of his vehicle.

Suddenly there was a stuttering burst of machine gun fire from a hidden weapon. The rounds slammed into the ground near Fetterman, kicking splashes of dirt and water. That was joined by a half-dozen AKs firing on full-auto.

The moment the shooting started, Gerber dropped to his belly. With his thumb he flipped off the safety, but didn't return fire. No targets were visible.

The enemy machine gun, probably an RPD, was well hidden among the hootches and fences of the ville. He turned toward the direction where Fetterman had seen the enemy soldier, but there was no movement there, either.

Then Fetterman opened fire, squeezing off single-shots by jerking the trigger. Gerber saw the rounds hit the oil drum, kicking off great clouds of rust. The firing from the enemy increased, the rounds snapping through the air overhead.

Gerber spotted a muzzle-flash in the darkened doorway of a hootch and turned on it. He flipped his weapon's selector to full-auto and burned through the magazine in four short bursts. Firing from the hootch ceased.

Then the enemy appeared. Twelve of them ran along the road, crouched as if in a high wind. The attacking VC and NVA were shouting and shooting as they ran. Gerber rolled to his left into the corner of a rice paddy and aimed over the top. Now back on single-shot, he aimed at the enemy, firing slowly, deliberately.

His second round struck an enemy in the chest. The man threw his weapon to the ground as if in disgust. He looked at the stain spreading on his chest and then sat down before toppling onto his side.

Gerber whipped around and triggered a round at another running target. The man stumbled, regained his balance and screamed. Gerber fired again. The enemy spun and dropped facedown.

On the right, Fetterman was firing quickly in short bursts. He hit one VC in the stomach, dropping him. A second man brought his weapon to bear on Fetterman, but the master sergeant cut him down quickly. Dirt flew from the man's uniform as the rounds struck him.

Then as quickly as they attacked, the enemy retreated. As if on command, they turned and fled together, sprinting from the field and diving for cover among the hootches, oxcarts and fifty-five-gallon drums. The RPD kept up its chatter, the rounds whipping through the air over everyone's head. Thompson's jeep rocked on its springs as the slugs slammed into its side.

Gerber stopped firing as the enemy disappeared. A moment later the RPD fell silent, and there was no sound around them except a ringing echo that diminished quickly. Gerber looked left and right and saw that both Fetterman and Albright had survived the assault unhurt.

"Captain," said Albright, "we can get out to the south. The road swings around before we reach the river and we can get back to Duc Hoa."

"And leave what, fifteen, twenty enemy soldiers behind us?"

Albright looked over the jeep again and then back at the body of Thompson.

"Tony, what do you think?"

"They've got the position and the numbers. It's their ground and their contact. We're hanging it all out here."

Gerber shifted around again, his eyes on the village. The simple solution was to call in artillery and let the cannon-cockers destroy the area. Except that artillery rarely was effective against troops who were dug in. The only people who would suffer would be the villagers who, if they were still around, might be killed. And if they weren't, they would only have the rubble of their village to come back to.

"Albright, how fast can we get a company of strikers in here?"

Albright looked at his watch and then at the sun. It was late afternoon. "If we can get aviation support, probably inside of thirty minutes."

"Then I suggest you get on the horn and arrange it. Tell them we're in contact now, but the enemy can slip away if they don't hurry. If they land north of the ville, then we can act as a blocking force."

"Only three of us, Captain," said Fetterman, "and we've used quite a bit of our ammo."

"Then they can break the last ship off to drop eight or ten guys with us and to bring us more ammo." Gerber checked the time and added, "Let's get on with it. We mustn't be here after dark."

Albright nodded. "Yes, sir." He grabbed the handset and keyed it.

MORROW REREAD HER MEMO, lifting the top of the sheet off the rear of the typewriter so that she could see it. She realized that it was a mishmash of incoherent thoughts that led to an indistinct conclusion. She understood why she had been unable to convince Hodges that something was happening. With reasoning as faulty as that displayed, and with almost no evidence to speak of, her conclusions just didn't follow.

She let go of it and rocked back in her chair. How could she put her gut feeling onto paper? Her belief that something was going to happen soon wasn't based on actual evidence. It was based on her observations of Major Hobbs and her belief that nothing had happened to destroy the enemy. They hadn't had a major victory, but then there hadn't been a major defeat. There were skirmishes and small battles, but nothing that could be called destructive.

No, her memo didn't bring that out. It merely indicated, in a disjointed fashion, that she was bothered by the situation as it now stood. She knew that something was going to happen, but she couldn't prove it.

She jerked the paper out of the typewriter and smiled at the sound. Her typing teacher in high school would have flunked her for abusing the equipment, but who cared? No one worried about abusing the reporters. No one worried about the reporter's feelings.

She wadded the paper into a tight ball and threw it at a wastebasket halfway across the floor. It hit the rim and bounced up onto a vacant desk. She smiled at that and tried to figure out why she felt sick to her stomach.

Leaning forward, she opened the bottom drawer of her desk and pawed through it, but could find nothing of interest. She wasn't even sure what she was looking for. She wanted to scream. She wanted to cry, and she didn't know why.

Mark Hodges emerged from his cubicle and spotted her. As he turned toward her, she groaned inwardly because the last thing she wanted was to argue with him again. She shot a glance over her shoulder but could see no avenue of escape.

Hodges parked a hip on the edge of her desk. In one hand he clutched a sheet of paper as if it were some kind of talisman. He stared at her. "Where's your Green Beret friend?"

She felt suddenly dizzy. Her stomach flipped over, and she thought she was going to throw up. "Why?"

"We've gotten word from MACV that a Special Forces soldier was killed earlier today in the Duc Hue area west of here."

Morrow grabbed at the paper and scanned the four lines printed there. It mentioned nothing that would help her, except a cryptic line about Duc Hoa. It seemed the man was assigned to the unit there, but had died near Duc Hue.

"I don't think this is Gerber. He wasn't assigned to an A-Detachment."

"Yeah, I thought not. I figured if it had been him, there would have been more on it."

Morrow read the message again. "I told you things were beginning to pick up."

"This is nothing," said Hodges.

"Nothing? A man is dead. I hardly think that is nothing."

"That's not what I mean," said Hodges, "and you know it. I mean that a single soldier killed in an ambush doesn't mark the beginning of something new."

Morrow rubbed her face exasperatedly with both her hands. "Have you ever had a hunch?"

"Of course," said Hodges. He chuckled to himself and added, "I've had dozens of them. Some have actually been right. Those that were right were based on fact and information. It wasn't something that I made up out of whole cloth."

"Well, neither is this. I'm telling you that something is beginning here, and if we don't keep our eyes open, we're going to miss it until it falls on us."

Hodges stood. "Robin, why don't you go on home? Get some rest. Take tomorrow off and then come back in. See if everything looks as gloomy."

"Christ, Hodges, this isn't like it's something that's wrong with me. I'm telling you how it is out there and you just ignore it."

Now Hodges shook his head. He looked at Morrow and then turned as someone burst into the city room. Hodges saw the man heading for his office and said, "Hey! I'm over here."

The newcomer turned, approached rapidly and handed him another sheet ripped from the teletype machine. Hodges scanned it and handed it to Morrow.

When she finished reading it, she said, "See?"

"This has nothing to do with anything else. A missing helicopter doesn't mean enemy action. It only means that a helicopter is missing."

"Come on, Mark," said Robin. "First we have a man killed and then almost immediately learn that a helicopter is missing. The action is picking up."

"Tomorrow, Robin," said Hodges, "I'll want you to get out to Song Be and see if anything new has been learned about the missing chopper. Get everything you can and then get back here."

"Then you're attaching some importance to this?"

"Nothing other than the fact that there was a crew of four Americans on board and, according to this, one American passenger. Five men are missing, and the way things are going here, that's the big news."

"Song Be?" she asked.

"Yeah. Special Forces camp there. You know any of them?"

She nodded. "Yeah, I know some of them. Captain Bromhead is the detachment commander. If he knows anything, he'll fill me in on it."

"Then go out there and find out what's happening."

Morrow stood up, the sick feeling still bubbling in her stomach. "I will," she said.

7

SONG BE SPECIAL
FORCES CAMP B-34

The first of the two patrols had formed near the front gate. The Special Forces NCOs had used the time to check the equipment while they waited for Bromhead to reappear from the commo bunker. The NCOs had circulated among the strikers, making sure the canteens were full, that each man had all the spare ammo he required and that each man had his share of the squad equipment. They discovered that one of the men had thrown away the spare batteries, and Bocker had to run back to the commo bunker to get a couple more.

While Bocker retrieved the batteries, Bromhead left the radio and walked up the short flight of stairs and stepped into the bright afternoon light. He stopped and looked at the men standing near the gate. He walked over to the patrol to wait until Bocker returned.

"Okay, Galvin," he said, "don't press it too hard tonight. You've got only four or five hours of light left. I doubt you'll get much outside the range of our big mortars. Play it by ear and don't push it."

"Yes, sir."

"And remember, we'll have another patrol out there as well, so don't get trigger-happy."

"Yes, sir."

"The odds are that Justin's helicopter is down more than fifty miles from here. The choppers from Cu Chi and Tay Ninh will probably locate the aircraft before you do."

"I understand that, Captain, but we've got to do something."

"Yes," responded Bromhead, thinking about what Mildebrandt had said. He studied the older man. Bocker was fairly big, but his hair was thinning and starting to go gray. There were deep lines around his eyes and on his forehead. Bromhead knew that Bocker had two daughters at home, and a wife who didn't understand why her husband had to go to Vietnam when the husbands of other wives stayed in garrison in the World for years on end.

Finally Bromhead pulled him to the side. "Galvin, I think this is a futile gesture. We'd be better off to wait for the choppers, then make an aerial search. Keep everyone on standby here until we have something to go on." He saw that Bocker was going to protest and held up his hand to stop him. "No, go on out. Who knows what might happen? But I don't want you taking any chances. I don't want to get anyone killed for no good reason."

"Captain, I don't want to sit on my hands around here. If I can get into the field, I might learn something."

Bromhead slapped Bocker on the shoulders. "Okay, I read you. Make normal radio checks. Keep it slow and easy and don't get too far to the west tonight."

"I've done this before."

"Right."

Together they moved closer to the patrol. The other Special Forces NCO, Staff Sergeant Alvin Wright, was waiting patiently. He was a thin man with black hair and almost no lines on his face. If it hadn't been for the fact that he was a staff sergeant in the Special Forces, everyone would have thought Wright was a high school student.

"Let's get them going," said Bocker.

Wright nodded and waved a hand. The point man broke away from the group. He ran through the gate, then loped down the road that led to the edge of the runway. Keeping to the side of the peta-prime, he circled back to the west, outside the perimeter wire. As he moved across the short grass, cut down for the killing fields around the camp, he slowed, then followed a path to the jungle, which he entered. As he disappeared, there was a screech, and a giant red bird windmilled out of the trees, swooped toward the ground and then began a fluttering climb.

The patrol followed the point, spreading out, with Bocker at the rear. Just before he entered the jungle, he turned and took a final look at the camp. In the distance a helicopter was approaching, and Bocker figured that either Bromhead or Mildebrandt would climb on board for the aerial search. For a moment he wished he had waited. Then he realized that waiting wasn't always the answer.

He stepped between two tall teak trees and noticed that the light had changed from the bright afternoon sun to a diffuse green glow that filtered through the trees to the ground. He moved deeper into the jungle, and the light faded. It was dim around him. The ground under his feet turned mushy, and he could hear water dripping somewhere.

"Yeah," he mumbled, "maybe the captain was right."

AT FIRST THERE WAS ONLY a quiet popping in the distance. Gerber scanned the horizon and finally spotted the flight of ten helicopters as it came at them. In the past twenty minutes, while Albright had worked the radio, Fetterman and Gerber had kept their eyes on the village of Ap Tan Hoa Four. Since the enemy soldiers there had made the abortive assault on them, there had been no activity.

Gerber shifted slightly, taking the weight off his left side. He lay behind a rice paddy dike, his weapon pointed at the village. The sun had slipped lower in the sky, and the weather wasn't as hot as it had been. Gerber was thirsty, but refused to get out his canteen. Instead, he ignored his discomfort and kept his attention focused on the ville.

As the choppers came closer, the radio burst into life. From his position near the jeep, Albright crawled to it and snatched the handset off the passenger seat. He stood up, saw the helicopters and then dropped to one knee. He spoke quietly, the words barely audible.

The aircraft turned slightly and began a long descent. None of them broke from the formation. Gerber cast a puzzled look in Albright's direction. He whispered that they were maintaining unit integrity. The whole flight would touch down near them with the reinforcements and ammo they had requested.

Gerber nodded and turned back to watch the choppers. One ship left the formation, dived to the ground, hovered along it and then broke to the right, climbing rapidly. As it pulled up, a smoke grenade tumbled from the rear. It struck the ground, bounced and then began billowing yellow smoke.

The flight got closer. The noise from the choppers drifted across the village. When they were near the ground, they flared, almost in unison. As the skids leveled, the door guns remained silent. The gunships whipping along the sides of the flight didn't fire. Everyone was waiting for the enemy to appear.

Then, just before the helicopters touched ground, one of them broke from the flight, crossing in front of it and spewing great clouds of smoke. The aircraft turned up on the side and swung around so that Gerber lost sight of the helicopters. He had never realized how effective Smoky could be.

Seconds later the aircraft touched down and then lifted off, climbing to the north away from the village. Still there was no shooting. The enemy, hidden among the hootches and cover of Ap Tan Hoa Four, refused to come out to fight.

As the smoke dissipated, a line of men moved forward. They swept across the open field on line, and as they approached the village they began to disappear from sight.

Gerber's attention was drawn away as the flight turned again, coming toward them. It set up behind them. Again the smoke ship broke away and began to spray a gray-white cloud that obscured the village. Just as the cloud began to settle to the ground, a single aircraft dropped from the rear of the formation. It touched down near the jeeps. As the skids hit the road, the men leaped to the ground and the helicopter took off in a cloud of swirling dust and smoke.

One of the men ran around the rear of the jeep and fell to the rice paddy beside Gerber. He glanced at the village that was just becoming visible again.

"What you got?"

"Maybe two dozen VC and NVA. Haven't seen them since they rushed us."

There was a single shot, but it came from an M-16. The men that Gerber could see on the outskirts of the village dived for cover. A cloud of red appeared on the main street. Gerber figured that one of the strikers had thrown a smoke grenade, but there was still no return fire. A moment later the sweep began again, the men moving slowly now, staying close to the cover that was available.

A burst ripped through the quiet, but it sounded like an M-60 machine gun and not a Russian-made RPD. The American who had talked to Gerber crawled away, heading toward the jeep. He whispered something to Albright and then grabbed the handset from the radio. He spoke into it, nodded and then called back.

"Our guys are getting a little trigger-happy. They haven't found the enemy."

"They didn't walk out," said Gerber, "and the ground looks too wet and soft to hold much in the way of a tunnel complex."

There was a single explosion from a grenade, but Gerber couldn't see where it had detonated. He rolled to his left just as the roof of a hootch collapsed, the dirt swirling upward. From it came a sustained burst that sounded like ripping cloth. Several strikers returned fire, their rounds punching into the mud wall.

A moment later the weapon flew out the door, and a lone man, dressed only in black pajama shorts, followed it, his hands in the air. He had taken only three steps when a shot from the rear dropped him. As he fell, the strikers opened fire on another hootch. That was returned sporadically. One of the strikers began to crawl forward. He disappeared into a depression, and a moment later one arm and shoulder appeared as he threw a grenade.

The hootch blew up with a muffled roar. The roof fell in and one wall collapsed in a cloud of red dust. The explosion exposed two men. Gerber aimed at one, but before he could pull the trigger one of them threw down his rifle and staggered into the open. He fell to his knees and then onto his stomach.

The second man didn't move until someone appeared in the door of the hootch. Then he tried to shoot, but the striker was too fast. The burst lifted the man off his feet and slammed him into a wall. He slid down it slowly as the striker leaped toward him, jerking the AK from his hands.

There was a wild burst of firing on the east side of the ville. The RPD opened up, supported by a couple of AKs. Green tracers struck the ground and tumbled harmlessly upward. The firing increased as more weapons joined it. Then came the answer from the Americans and the strikers. The sound of M-16s, M-60s and M-79s combined into a single, long detonation that washed out all other noise. Dirt and smoke drifted over the battlefield.

Slightly to the north of where he crouched, Gerber noticed a half-dozen enemy soldiers appear. They were trying vainly to keep their heads down, and this was exactly what Gerber had anticipated. He waited as the fleeing men came closer, then yelled for them to halt. One of them did, dropping his AK, but the others simply opened fire. Their shots were wild, kicking up dirt near Gerber and Fetterman and the strikers with them. The strikers returned fire, killing two NVA soldiers. A third tried to flee into the swamps but was cut down. The rest of the men dropped their weapons and lifted hands in surrender.

Gerber got to his feet and moved toward the enemy soldiers. When he reached them, he ordered them to get down, spread their arms and legs and lie still.

By now, firing in the village had begun to taper off. The M-16s were hammering away, but the AKs and the RPD had fallen silent. Gerber took cover near the side of an old oxcart as the strikers maneuvered toward a hootch. When they were close, they used grenades, blowing off the roof and then dropping two of the walls. They poured more rounds into the smoking rubble until one of the Americans ordered them to cease fire.

A silence descended on the village. The men formed again and began a quick sweep, searching for the enemy. They poked into the hootches that were still standing, opened the family bunkers and kicked over stacks of loose lumber or piles of gourds. They opened the water buffalo pens and searched through them carefully. Occasionally they would find something: a couple of rifles wrapped in heavy cloth, or ammunition in tin cans that required an opener to get at the bullets.

A Special Forces lieutenant approached Gerber, and his gaze fell on the two men spread-eagled on the ground. "What you got?"

"Prisoners. We'd better get them into camp. See if we can get some answers."

The lieutenant looked at the enemy soldiers and then at the body of Thompson. Albright had dragged the body closer to the jeep. Gerber could see the lieutenant's jaw muscles working. There was hate in his eyes, and his finger tightened on the trigger of his weapon.

Gerber stepped toward the young officer. "If you kill them, we won't find out what happened here. They'll be nothing but dead soldiers. We keep them alive and we'll be able to hurt the enemy more."

Still the lieutenant kept his eyes on the two enemy soldiers. He moved the barrel of his weapon toward them slowly, as if thinking it over. Gerber wanted to step in and stop him, but knew that any movement might set him off.

"Lieutenant, think it over."

"They won't talk. They won't say a word. They never do."

"Look at them," ordered Gerber. "These aren't hard-core regulars. They're not fanatics from the North. We handle this right and we'll get a lot of information out of them."

The lieutenant tore his eyes from the two men and looked up at Gerber. "You sure, sir?"

"I'm positive. A live soldier can tell us many things, but a dead one is just that—dead."

"All right, Captain." He pointed at Albright. "Get these guys tied up and prepare them for travel. Check them for weapons."

"Yes, sir."

The men were all on their feet then. Fetterman had moved from his position and picked up Thompson's body. He placed it in the rear of one of the jeeps.

"Sir," said the lieutenant, "the choppers are on call and we can have them back whenever we want."

"You satisfied with the sweep through the ville?"

The lieutenant turned and studied Ap Tan Hoa behind him. He stared at it for thirty seconds or more and then nodded. "Given the time of day and the fact that we got the enemy, yes, I'm satisfied."

"Then whistle up the choppers and let's get out of here."

"Thompson's jeep can't be driven," Albright informed Gerber.

"Then destroy it."

"Captain," said Fetterman, "you want to fly back or go in the jeep."

"I want to stay with the prisoners."

"Yes, sir. I'll go back with Sergeant Albright. We'd like a couple of strikers."

"Sure. Listen, we'll get Thompson's jeep rigged for destruction. You guys get out of here now while it's still light."

"Yes, sir."

IT WAS LATE AFTERNOON when Lockridge and Jones and their dates left the house. They had spent most of the afternoon in the living room with its partially boarded bay window, listening to the records that had come from the American PX. The thing that bothered Jones was that nearly all of them were still sealed in their shrink wrap. They hadn't been opened and hadn't been played. Le Tran explained that most of them were gifts from other GIs and that she didn't like to play them alone.

Lockridge raised his eyebrows. "That mean you don't bring them home?"

Le Tran lowered her eyes coyly. "You are the very first to come here."

"Well," said Lockridge happily. He moved closer and put his arm around her shoulders. He noticed that she stiffened briefly but then relaxed.

They all sat quietly for a few moments, listening to Jefferson Airplane and then to the Moody Blues. Lockridge thought that it was all crazy. Here he was sitting in a room furnished in a strange mixture of Western and Eastern styles, listening to music by American and English rock bands in the middle of a war zone. Tomorrow morning he would be on duty again, carrying a loaded weapon and waiting to shoot at Vietnamese, but this evening he was in the home of a beautiful Vietnamese woman. He felt himself stir with desire for her. Not love, he told himself, because she was Vietnamese, but lust. He lusted after her body, but she wasn't the girl that he would take home to his mother.

Almost as if she had read his thoughts, she stood and walked over to the record player. As she turned it off, she said, "You will take us to dinner now? A nice place with low lights and soft music?"

Jones shot a glance at Lockridge, telling him that he didn't want to spend a pile of money. Lockridge ignored the look because his goal was in sight. He knew that if he spent enough money on her, she would feel obligated to be nice to him.

"Do you have something special in mind?" he asked.

She spun and clapped her hands. "Yes. Something very nice, but it will not be expensive. I know you do not have much money, even for a rich American."

"Not all Americans are rich."

"You earn more in one month than a Vietnamese can earn in a whole year of hard labor." There was a flicker behind her eyes, but Lockridge didn't know if it was envy or anger. She added, "You have so very much and the Vietnamese have so very little."

"You seem to have a nice house here."

"Upstairs there are holes in the roof and broken windows that we cannot fix. There is only one bed. My sister and I take turns. She uses it one night and I get it the next."

Lockridge hoped that it was Le Tran's night for the bed, but didn't say anything.

"We work for a month for very little money, enough to feed us and buy us clothes. There is never anything left over."

Lockridge nodded slowly as if he was beginning to understand what she was telling him.

"We apply for jobs at your bases, but the applications are always turned down. We do not know the palms to grease. We do not know how to get the jobs that will pay us a year's wages in a single month."

Here comes the pitch, Lockridge thought.

But instead Le Tran said, "So we give it up. We find other ways to earn money, but there is never enough."

And then Lockridge understood completely. Le Tran and her sister didn't want a job at an American base. Neither believed that Lockridge or Jones could get them employment. The sisters had taken to the street to earn money in the world's oldest profession. Lockridge, who had claimed repeatedly that he had never paid for it in his life, suddenly found himself facing a good-looking woman who would ask him to pay for it. Her approach was subtle, bordering on the brilliant, but she was a whore, pure and simple.

For a moment Lockridge considered ways of getting out of the situation and then realized that he didn't want to. Her admission took some of the excitement out of the evening because he knew that they would end up in bed. And then he decided it didn't matter because that was exactly what he wanted and he could now relax a little. He didn't have to be charming. He just had to have money.

8

**THE JUNGLE EAST OF
AN LOC NEAR THE SONG
BE RIVER**

Sergeant Justin Tyme came awake slowly. He was aware that it was dark, damp and hot. His body ached. He didn't open his eyes right away because he was listening to everything that was going on around him. To one side were quiet voices speaking English. And he knew that he was lying on something wet. He remembered the enemy bullets ripping into the side of the chopper and remembered it diving toward the trees. Then the world had turned to darkness.

He opened his eyes and saw that it wasn't quite as dark as he had thought. There were the last slanting rays of the sun filtering through the thick jungle around him. He could see two men to the right, both crouched behind a fallen tree, staring into the jungle, M-16s in their hands.

With an effort that sent pain through his whole body, he sat up. He wiped a hand across his sweat-damp face and rubbed the perspiration on his fatigue jacket. He felt like an old man with pain in his joints. Ignoring that, he stood swaying for a moment as a curtain of black descended and then rose. He took a step forward and felt a hand grab him near the elbow.

"You better sit down."

Slowly he turned and saw the crew chief standing next to him. "What happened?"

"We crashed into the trees. You were knocked out. Gave us a scare, your being unconscious for so long. Look, sit down and I'll get you some water."

"Why are we still here?"

"Lost the radios. Survival radio isn't working, either. Dumb Peter Pilot dropped it into the water as he was unassing the aircraft. Idiot."

Tyme felt suddenly weak. He reached out to steady himself. The crew chief helped him to the cargo compartment and had him sit down.

"We need to get out of here."

"Can't do it. Or couldn't. Not with you unconscious and the door gunner hurt. We couldn't carry you and we couldn't leave you."

"We've got to get away from the chopper because the VC will find us."

The crew chief took a canteen from under his seat and opened it. He handed it to Tyme. "Sip the water. Not too much right away."

"I know." Tyme lifted the canteen to his lips and drank slowly. He filled his mouth with water, sloshed it around and then swallowed it. Incongruously the thought came to him that only in the movies did men caught in the jungle spit out water.

When he finished, he capped the canteen and repeated, "We need to get away from here."

"We're probably better off staying," said the crew chief. "There'll be people looking for us, and they have a better chance of finding us if we don't stray too far from here."

Tyme stood up again and felt his strength returning. "Where's my weapon?"

Again the crew chief reached under his seat. "Right here. Kept it safe for you."

"Good." He checked it, then made sure the safety was on. "Now why haven't we been found?"

"That's a good question. We've seen a couple of helicopters fly over, but without radios we couldn't contact them. We popped smoke, but they didn't see it."

"Didn't you get a distress call out?"

"One of the first rounds hit the bundle of cables under the cargo compartment and that severed the radios from the antenna. AC made his call in the blind, but we didn't receive any acknowledgment. After the Peter Pilot dropped the survival radio in the water, we weren't able to raise anyone."

Tyme shook his head. "I thought you guys were a little sharper than that. Christ, what a boondoggle."

The crew chief shrugged helplessly. "What can I say? This was a DSC mission. We don't expect enemy action during them. We should've been better prepared, but this is the first time we've had the DSC ship downed by the enemy."

Tyme rubbed both his eyes. "Even if we don't move far from the crash site, we've got to get away from the aircraft. Charlie will be looking for it, and if we stay here he'll have an easy time getting to us."

"All right. I'll get the AC over and you can talk to him."

"We don't have a lot of time. It'll be dark in a little while and we should get set before then."

The crew chief nodded grimly and moved off. Tyme noticed that he didn't seem to have much knowledge of the jungle. He made noise as he walked, stepping on small plants just beginning to fight their way into the thick carpet of rotting vegetation. If the enemy moved through the area, they would find all kinds of signs that someone had been there. Apart from the remains of the downed chopper, the ground around it was littered with trash—bits of cardboard from C-ration containers, paper, cigarette butts and empty cans, a few scattered rounds and a paperback novel. These guys were treating all this as if it were a walk through the woods and they didn't give a shit about littering.

Tyme sat down again and rubbed his head. There was a pounding behind his eyes and a roaring in his ears. His eyes weren't working quite right. It was like looking through a long tunnel, and he had no peripheral vision. He knew that he had a concussion and wondered how bad it was and if he was in any danger. The faster he could get out, the better off he would be, but there didn't seem to be any prospect of getting out before morning.

Two men appeared out of the growing dark. One was the crew chief and the other a pilot, the AC. Tyme noticed that the pilot was a tall, thin man with light brown hair who looked about fifteen years old.

"You have a problem?" asked the man.

Tyme saw the bars of a warrant officer sewn to the collar of the man's jungle fatigues. The black bars were little more than a dark smudge in the advancing darkness, but the gold thread of the bars was visible.

"No problem, sir," said Tyme. "I was telling your crew chief—"

"Sergeant Stanfield."

"Sergeant Stanfield, that we'd better move off. If Charlie saw us go down, he's going to be moving in on us tonight. We've got to get out of here."

The warrant officer stood for a moment, staring into the thick green jungle almost as if he could see something in it. There was a rustling of wind through the leaves, a call of a bird and the scream of a monkey.

"How far?"

"Couple of hundred meters would be good. Give us enough of a cushion so that we could E and E if we had to, then we could get back here in the morning."

"Okay, Sergeant. That sounds good. We'll get on it."

"Yes, sir. I'd also like to suggest that we take as much of the equipment with us in case Charlie finds the chopper. We don't want to give him anything."

"Yeah. Stanfield, get your gear together. I'll take care of everything up front." He stood up and then looked at Tyme. "What about the radio control heads?"

"If you can get them out, take them. If not, make sure you zero out the frequencies."

"I'm smart enough to do that," snapped the pilot.

"Yes, sir," said Tyme. He hesitated. "We should hold it down, too. Sound travels a long way in the jungle, and it can lead back to us."

The pilot seemed to bristle for a moment, as if he wanted to retort to the smartass sergeant, then realized that Tyme was right. He nodded and climbed into the cockpit of the helicopter, using a survival knife to twist the quick-release screws on the radios.

Tyme got up and walked around the downed chopper, studying it. There was so much that could be used by the enemy, so much that Charlie could use in his war effort. Even the metal skin of the aircraft could be useful. And the battery in the nose of the chopper, which weighed eighty pounds, was something the enemy would love to find. There was no way for the Americans to destroy it without making noise, and it was too heavy for them to carry away.

The AC reappeared, holding up the small control heads. "You want to find us a place to hole up?" He was leaning close to Tyme and had kept his voice low.

"Be happy to, sir."

"Good. We'll be ready in ten minutes."

Tyme nodded. He checked his weapon again, glanced around and then moved into the trees near the rear of the helicopter. It was the roughest terrain. They would have to step around trees and bushes and crawl under fallen trees. If Charlie tried to follow, especially in the coming night, he would have to make some noise. That would give them a warning. It made the whole thing perfect. Tyme eased forward until he found a good spot for them to hide until the sun came up and they could hope for rescue.

SANTINI STOOD on the east side of the helipad, waiting for a chopper. Behind him was the airfield of Nha Trang where jets and propeller-driven aircraft landed and took off. Standing next to him, clutching his hands, was Co, the young Vietnamese woman he'd first seen earlier tied to a chair.

The sun was gone, and he stood next to a fifty-five-gallon drum filled with trash, paper and wood that could become a

landing light if the base electricity failed. Now there were four
blue lights burning, one on each corner of the rubberized pad.
In the dim light, Santini could almost see the symbol, a copy
of the patch worn by members of the First Aviation Brigade,
painted in the center.

In the distance he heard the pop of rotor blades and the roar
of the turbine engine. He stepped to the rear, down a slight
slope and away from the pad. The woman moved closer to him,
holding tighter, afraid.

Santini looked at her and thought of his sister at home. He
doubted that this woman, this girl, was much older than his
sister. He felt his heart turn over as he thought again about how
she had been treated by her own countrymen, and was ap-
palled at the torture.

"It's all right," he said. "The helicopter will be here in a
moment."

He smiled at her and thought about the argument he'd had
with Major Madden. The major had wanted to turn her over
to the MPs just as soon as they could. Santini had argued with
him for nearly forty minutes, finally convincing Madden that
they should take her out to one of the Special Forces camps,
let the men know her background and have her imprisoned
there. It was the best compromise because it got her away from
the Vietnamese at Nha Trang, who seemed to think of her as
a plaything rather than an enemy soldier.

Santini had then taken her to the PX and watched as she had
moved among the items for sale, afraid to touch anything. He
had finally convinced her that it wasn't a trick of some kind
and that she should select some clothes for herself. She had
then changed from a suspected Vietcong to a girl suddenly told
to pick out a new wardrobe.

Walking among the clothes, sometimes feeling the material, she would take something from the rack, hold it against
herself, then put it back. In this manner she had orbited the
clothing section where women's clothes hung for GIs who
wanted to find presents for their local girlfriends.

Finally she had found something that she'd liked, and Santini had escorted her to the front so that they could pay for it.

Afterward, he had taken her to the NCO Club and bought her dinner. They had eaten slowly, then gone back to the Fifth Special Forces Headquarters where they had waited for nightfall and the chopper that would take them to the camp.

Now they stood together near the helipad. As the noise from the chopper changed from a dull popping of the rotor blades and the insectile buzz of the turbine to a loud roar punctuated by the rotor system, Santini moved farther down the hillside. He bent his head, holding his beret on with his right hand while the girl clung to his left.

A light stabbed out, illuminating the pad, and then the chopper settled to the ground. As the skids touched the rubberized pad, the landing light went out. The red and green navigation lights blinked in the dark and the red anticollision beacon rotated in the rear.

Santini started forward, ducking as the wash from the rotors tore at him. He felt a tug at his hand and saw that the girl was frightened now. He smiled and yelled over the noise of the chopper, "It's okay. No one's going to hurt you. Come on."

She hesitated for another moment, staring upward at the massive machine with its men dressed in strange costumes and large helmets trailing black cords. She didn't want anything to do with them.

But then Santini was pulling on her hand, dragging her up the hill closer to the chopper. The winds increased as they approached the helicopter. She closed her eyes and let Santini pull her along because she trusted him.

They reached the side of the aircraft, and she stepped up on the skid. Santini grabbed her around the waist and lifted her as she ducked her head. She stood still, with her head bent, touching the top of the cargo compartment. Santini climbed in and pulled her to the troop seat. When she sat down, Santini reached around her and buckled her in.

Almost before they were set, the chopper picked up to a hover. It sat there for a moment, then spun to the right, charging across the ground as it lifted upward. When the ground dropped away, the girl grabbed Santini's arm.

She looked out the open cargo compartment door for a few minutes and then leaned against Santini, her eyes closed. He grinned and held on to her.

The flight was short. Within minutes they were on the ground again. As the chopper landed, two men came out of hiding in the bunker line. Santini helped the girl from the helicopter, and as soon as they were on the ground and clear of the aircraft, it lifted off. The pilots had been told not to remain on the ground for very long after dark.

One of the men came forward and shook Santini's hand. "Welcome to our camp. This the prisoner?"

"Let's not think of her as a prisoner. I think the whole situation is a little suspect. We've got a chance to develop a real ally."

"Okay, Santini, have it your way. Come on in and we'll get both of you settled."

"Thanks. You've got me scheduled out tomorrow?"

"Manifested through on the morning chopper. That's usually here about ten. That suit you?"

"That's fine."

The man slapped Santini on the shoulder. "And we've taken the liberty of plugging you into the watch system. You have the midnight-to-four."

Santini had to laugh. "Delightful."

"When you're understrength and the people at Nha Trang want a visit, they have to work."

"I'll warn everyone."

GERBER AND FETTERMAN sat in the back of the room while three of the Special Forces men of Duc Hoa interrogated the prisoners. It wasn't a rough questioning with bamboo under the fingernails. It was a quick firing of questions in French, English and Vietnamese, not giving the men time to think or time to answer. It was a relentless grilling. The three interrogators moved around the two prisoners, shouting at them, talking to them, arguing with them. And when they seemed on the verge of collapse, or one put his head down to rest, the three Americans swooped in, jerking him upright.

One of the ammo bunkers had been hurriedly cleaned out so it could be used as the interrogation room. Two chairs had been set back to back in the center of wooden-plank flooring. The two Vietnamese sat in the chairs at a modified position of attention. There were two lamps on the floor, one shining into the face of one man and the other into the face of the second. Everything else had been removed so that the two men would have nothing to look at.

The three Americans were dressed in jungle fatigues. The sleeves of each were rolled to halfway between the elbow and shoulder. They were sweaty men, who had been at it for nearly two hours. Their voices had become husky in the time they had been in the bunker, but they didn't stop. Another sergeant brought them beers, which they consumed while the prisoners watched. It was all part of the psychological warfare they were conducting against the two men.

Listening, Gerber and Fetterman stood near the door outside the circle of light created by the lamps. Fetterman had wanted to direct the interrogation, having seen Kepler from his old team do it a number of times, but Gerber had stopped him.

"This is their show," he had said. "Let them run it their own way."

Fetterman had understood the wisdom of that. It had been their friend who had been ambushed and killed. It was their duty to find the men who had done it and exact retribution.

Gerber finally tired of watching the interrogation. It looked more like a group of teachers ganging up on two wayward students, shouting at them and threatening them, but with both parties knowing that nothing physical was going to happen. Only fatigue would break down the will of the prisoners and that could take hours, maybe days.

Then, just when he thought he would leave the ammo bunker for the cool comfort of the team house, one of the prisoners bent over, his hands on his face. There was a racking sob, followed by a wail and a sudden burst of rapid Vietnamese that was so incoherent no one could understand it.

Tet

One of the Special Forces NCOs leaped forward and jerked the other man to his feet. He was dragged from the ammo bunker and taken to another area to be held so that the remaining SF men could question the sobbing prisoner closely. They didn't want him drawing strength from his friend.

Captain Jewell came in, nodded at Gerber and Fetterman and then moved close. Albright whispered something to him, and the two men began a heated argument. Jewell made a move toward the prisoner, but Albright stopped him. Then Albright dropped to a knee in front of the Oriental and started talking to him slowly and quietly.

Jewell moved out of the circle of light and walked around its perimeter like a vulture waiting for something to die. As he flickered in and out of the shadows, the prisoner's eyes flashed toward him.

Finally Jewell slipped back to where Gerber and Fetterman waited. He leaned near them. "We've almost got it."

"It?" said Gerber.

"Yeah, the name of the man who organized the ambush. He wasn't with them when they cut down Thompson."

Fetterman turned so that he was facing Jewell, his body no more than six inches from the captain's. "Then you're going after him?"

Jewell had to smile. "In a guerrilla war you've got to keep the level of terror high. If we learn the name of the local Vietcong who ordered the ambush and he dies within hours of Thompson, it's going to make them all think twice about trying something else."

Gerber nodded his approval. "If you get a mission organized in the next couple of hours, I'd like to go along."

Jewell searched his face and asked, "Why? You didn't know Thompson."

"Because he was Special Forces and because of the way he was executed. He wasn't killed in battle but was shot in the back of the head at close range."

"Okay," said Jewell. He turned to Fetterman. "And you? You want to go, too?"

"Of course," said Fetterman. "We do this right and it'll make the local leaders think twice about helping the VC and about shooting prisoners in the back of the head."

Albright let out a whoop and spun. "We've got it," he said. "He spilled it all."

"Okay," said Jewell. "Okay. I want everyone to meet in five minutes in the team house. We'll decide what to do then. Take the prisoner out and put him with the first man."

For an instant Albright hesitated, as if wanting to shoot the man for his part in the death of Thompson. Instead, he reached out and lifted the man to his feet. With one hand on the VC's elbow, Albright guided the prisoner from the ammo bunker.

"There's going to be a fight about this," said Jewell. "Everyone's going to want to go on the mission. They'll be pissed that two outsiders are going to go."

"Tell them," said Gerber, "that each of them has a job to do here. As outsiders, we have the time to spare."

"That's going to piss them off even more," said Jewell. "That you don't think they have the time to spare."

"What I meant," said Gerber, "was that part of our job is to run these kinds of missions. Their job is training the Vietnamese here. I know how it sounds, but that job is important. We can do more damage to the enemy that way. Besides, we'll let it be known, after the mission, that more Special Forces men came from Saigon to exact retribution. Another terror tactic."

"Yeah," said Jewell. "I like that."

IT HAD BEEN A NIGHT to remember. Both Vietnamese girls had responded positively to the great dinner and the dancing. No cheap honky-tonk for them, either, only the best—dancing under the stars in the rooftop gardens of the Carasel Hotel. There had been many slow dances with Le Tran rubbing herself against Lockridge, molding her body to his with the promise of things to come.

And when they sat together in the dimness of a corner table, away from the lights of the bar and overlooking the neon of the streets below, the promise grew. Lockridge casually put his hand on her bare knee, and she opened herself with no urging from him. He slid his fingers up the smoothness of her thigh as she spread her legs a little more.

He glanced at the people on the dance floor, a swaying crowd of sweating men and women who seemed to have forgotten the music. Tall American men, in strange postures, their back-sides thrust outward, towered over the shorter, smaller Viet-namese women as they tried to dance cheek to cheek with them.

Lockridge kept his hand moving, describing circles on the flesh of Le Tran's thigh, moving it even higher. She still didn't protest as he finally reached his goal, a finger against her silk panties. Instead, she reached over and touched him lightly on the crotch. He wanted to rock back, his eyes closed while she solved his immediate problem, but was afraid that she would stop without his encouragement. He kissed her, his tongue in her mouth, his finger probing gently, insistently.

She shifted around, holding him and moaning quietly. She was ready now. He could tell easily, but there were too many people in the rooftop garden. There was too much light. But he tugged at the elastic of her panties, sliding his finger inside until she let go of him and buried her face in his neck, a pur-ring in her throat.

Paradise was so close, yet so far. Lockridge looked up and saw Jones and Le Tran's sister coming toward them. Reluc-tantly he straightened, drawing his hand free and letting it linger between her thighs as he pulled her skirt down so that the approaching couple wouldn't know what had been hap-pening.

When Jones and his date stopped at the table, the girl said, "It is time that we go home now."

Le Tran smiled, her eyes half-closed as if she was about to pass out. She nodded. "Yes. Home. You may come in for a cup of tea."

The thought of tea wasn't on Lockridge's mind. But then tea would get them in the door and that was all he cared about.

Surreptitiously he reached down to adjust his clothes so that he could stand up without embarrassment. He threw a handful of MPC on the table and then nearly dragged Le Tran downstairs to the street.

They hailed a cab, and as soon as they were in the back seat, Lockridge tried to slip his hand up Le Tran's skirt again. She shifted around, giving him the freedom to do it.

And then they were at the house. Lockridge tossed the money in the driver's window, for once not arguing with the price, which was much too high. He grinned at the driver and spun around. The house was ablaze with light.

"What's going on?" demanded Lockridge.

"My mother is here. She came for a visit."

Lockridge felt his shoulders slump, and he moaned in anguish. A mother in the house meant there would be nothing but tea.

Le Tran turned to him, leaned her head on his chest and let her hand wander over his crotch. "We can do nothing with my mother here. Nothing."

"I know," said Lockridge, his frustration mounting.

"You tell me your schedule and we can meet somewhere and have some fun."

Without a thought, Lockridge began to give her the entire schedule of the guards at the embassy, including the times the guards changed, when the slack periods were and how many men would be off each day of the Lunar New Year. He told her how she could sneak around the embassy to see him and where the most vulnerable points on the walls were. He told her everything he could remember, never thinking of the military value of the information he was handing out.

And there had been no protests from Jones this time because he was standing in the shadows, his hand inside the blouse of Le Tran's sister. His attention was drawn to the rock-hard points of her nipples as her tongue probed his mouth and her hand felt the swelling in his pants.

A light at the front of the house snapped on, and both couples jumped apart. An old Vietnamese woman, bent with age, appeared in the doorway and waited. Le Tran squeezed Lockridge's hand. "I shall see you soon."

"I know you will," said Lockridge, not knowing how soon it would be.

9

WIRE SERVICE BUREAU
CITY ROOM
DOWNTOWN SAIGON

Robin Morrow was only half-awake when she walked into the city room. The air was heavy with the aroma of coffee, and the air-conditioning was drying the sweat from her face and body quickly. She moved to her desk, and let her camera bag drop onto the floor, wishing someone would close the blinds on the windows. With a groan she sat in her chair, then leaned forward, her head in her hands. For some reason, she wished she was still in bed. It was just one of those days when it was too early to do anything.

As she sat there thinking about life in general and her place in it in particular, Mark Hodges left his office and moved among the desks, weaving his way toward her. He stopped short of her desk. "You okay?"

She looked up and blinked, as if seeing him for the first time in her life. "I'm fine. I'm just tired. I wish just once it wouldn't be so hot outside and so damned cold inside."

Hodges held out a piece of teletype paper. "This might make you feel better."

Without a word, she took the paper and scanned it. Marines at Khe Sanh had been attacked by a large force of Vietcong and NVA. They had been heavily mortared and rocketed, and it seemed that the enemy was trying to turn Khe Sanh into another Dien Bien Phu.

"Why should this make me happy?"

Hodges parked a hip on her desk and looked down at her. "You must really be in bad shape. This is the great battle that you predicted. You said the enemy was planning something, and this is it."

Morrow smiled weakly. "But."

"But," agreed Hodges. "This is their last gasp. They're trying for something spectacular so that when they hit the negotiating table, they'll have something to bargain with. Not much, but something."

"No," said Morrow. "This isn't it. This is the beginning, but this isn't what I've been worried about."

"Jesus, Robin. It looks like they've put all their eggs into one basket for this final attack. If the Marines beat it back, it's going to be all over but the shouting."

Morrow rocked back in her chair and studied her editor. Here was a man, she felt, who had no idea about what was happening. He made decisions, wrote articles about the war, expounded on his opinions, but had no idea what was going on around him. Maybe it was because he spent all his time in Saigon listening to career soldiers who had turned into politicians, telling him what he wanted to hear so that it would get printed at home. Men who were thinking of jobs after the Army and men who knew exactly what the President and his cabinet wanted to hear. Men who knew that high rank didn't come to those who rocked the boat.

But all that was garbage. Morrow knew it because she hung around with Mack Gerber and the lower ranking men at MACV Headquarters. Gerber had told her things he had observed on his trips into the field, not the classified observations that went into secret reports, but unclassified information that the media people didn't bother to ask for. Gerber had told her to read between the lines of reports, to see that the big battle in the Hobo Woods meant there were hundreds of enemy soldiers being infiltrated into the area. If the enemy had been abandoning the war, those men wouldn't have been there.

She sat up, opened a drawer, took out a tissue and slowly wiped the sweat from her face. Tossing the napkin into the wastebasket, she shook her head. "Mark, you don't understand. There's something big going down."

"Okay, Robin, have it your way." He straightened and looked at her as if she were a not-too-bright child who refused to listen to reason. "Since you won't listen to me, I want you to head over to the American embassy for the press briefing on this situation that's developing at Khe Sanh."

"What about Song Be?"

"That'll have to wait. Khe Sanh is more important now. That's why I want you over at the embassy."

"Wouldn't it make more sense for me to go to Khe Sanh in person?"

"Someone will cover that. Your job is to go to the embassy."

Morrow nodded and leaned forward. She could outline some of the things that Gerber had told her, but decided that Hodges wouldn't listen. She'd just have to wait until the situation blew up and it was too late for him to deny that it was happening. When the enemy made its move, she would have her story.

"What time's the briefing?" she asked wearily.

"At eleven. Take your camera and get us some good art. That building is fairly new, and we don't have any good pictures of it. Maybe we can work up a feature about it, if there's nothing else happening."

"You got your tickets yet?" she asked sarcastically.

"Ticket for what?"

Morrow stood. "Your ticket for the ride home. You must be leaving soon."

The look on Hodges's face hardened. "You just worry about yourself, Morrow."

"I'll be at the embassy in case anything important happens," she said sweetly.

THE ATTITUDE IN THE team house was one of expectation. Jewell had let his men interrogate the prisoners until they had every scrap of evidence they needed. They had learned as much as the two men knew and they were going to put it all to work for them. They had been lucky that the men they captured had been Vietcong from the local infrastructure and not NVA regulars who had come down from the North to assist the locals in their fight against the Americans. If the prisoners had been NVA, they wouldn't have known much that was useful.

Jewell sat on one of the tables in front of his men. "We've learned one thing that has been reported to Nha Trang in the past hour. That's the size of the NVA force now in our area. The increase is significant and suggests something is coming. There's going to be some kind of push by the enemy." He grinned at them and added, "No, I don't care to guess about it right now. Besides, that's not our immediate concern."

He pointed toward the rear of the room. "Now, for those of you who don't know, we have a couple of men in from SOG."

He waited while Gerber and Fetterman stood and then sat back down.

"All right. Here's what we know. Sergeant Thompson was on a normal swing through the countryside yesterday. Given the civic action programs demanded by MACV, and the fact that the area around here has been fairly quiet, Thompson was traveling alone in the middle of the day. Apparently the local infrastructure decided that his presence in a jeep by himself was too much of an insult. How can they control the population with lone American soldiers ranging far and wide?"

Jewell shifted his position and stared at the floor. He gripped the side of the table with both hands, the knuckles turning white. He swung his legs back and forth.

"Now apparently someone in one of the villages that Thompson passed through alerted the locals and they set up the ambush. They stopped his jeep outside of Ap Tan Hoa. He held them off until he was out of ammunition. They then advanced on him, took him prisoner and—"

Jewell's voice broke then, and he was quiet for a moment. No one in the small, dark, warm room spoke. A few watched the team commander as he fought to regain his control. They watched his chest heave and his breathing even out from the ragged gasps it had been. Each of them understood the emotion and none of them was embarrassed by it.

"They took him prisoner, shouting that he should surrender and he would be a prisoner. With no ammo, his radio shot to hell and his jeep disabled, he had no choice. He did as they advised and surrendered to them."

Again Jewell fell silent. He looked at his men. "From all appearances, they played the terror game with him. Held a pistol behind his head and fired it as he knelt there. A bullet into the ground or into the air. Thompson didn't react right. Seemed to be too brave. Maybe he believed they wouldn't really shoot him."

Now Jewell laughed, shaking his head. "I would have been shaking, but Thompson didn't even jump when the pistol was fired. A hell of a thing. Anyway, that pissed them off, so the leader shot him in the back of the head. Just like that. Killed him in violation of the rules of land warfare."

There was a moment of silence, then Jewell continued. "We know the name of the leader of the local cell—Tran Tri Van. I've seen him around the villages acting important. Some kind of elected local wheel and the head of the Vietcong infrastructure. Now no one's said that he pulled the trigger, but he's the leader and he's the one who's going to pay."

Jewell turned and picked up a photograph off the table beside him. He held it up. "Sergeant Thompson got this picture of the man several weeks ago. He's average, about five-five and about a 120 pounds. But he's easy to identify. He has a knife scar that runs across his face. The tip of his nose is missing."

"What are we going to do, Captain?" asked one of the men.

"I've spoken to a couple of you already and to our visitors. Because they were ambushed along with Sergeant Albright later, they've asked to go after Van. I've decided that they should."

"Captain," said another man, "I'd like to be included on that mission."

"Sorry, Prewitt, the team's been designed. Captain Gerber's made a good point. He suggested that he and Sergeant

Fetterman should be included because they're from Saigon.
Teaches the enemy that Special Forces soldiers from all over
Vietnam will come to avenge the death of a fellow.''

"He was my friend," said Prewitt.

"I know he was," said Jewell. "But listen to the plan. I
think you'll approve of it."

He waited for a minute, looking from face to face, trying to
gauge their reactions. He then launched into a detailed description of the plan based on information given to them by
the prisoner. Since it was something that was going to be carried out in the next few hours, it was decided that the prisoners would be held in a small hootch by themselves with no
contact with any of the Vietnamese except the camp commander. Once the mission was over, they would be put in with
the general POW population.

After he described the plan, he asked for questions. There
were a few, but most of the men realized that the plan was
good. Just a quick helicopter flight to Hiep Hoa and then a
quiet hike through the swamps until they were close to Ap Tan
Hoa Three where Van often spent the night. He was there
three or four nights a week, usually with two or three of his
most trusted soldiers and lately with the higher ranking
members of the NVA. The women there entertained them
through the night, and they often stayed until close to noon.

When Jewell ended the meeting, all the members of the team
talked to him privately, each explaining why he should be included on the team. Jewell told each of them why they weren't
going to be included, but that they must maintain a low profile so that the local Vietcong wouldn't report anything to their
superiors.

Gerber, Fetterman and Albright hung back until everyone
else was gone. Then all of them walked into the bright morning sun.

"How soon do you want to leave?" asked Jewell.

"It'll take us a couple of hours to get through the swamps,
but we don't want to leave too early. Get us a chopper in here
about one and then we'll head over to Hiep Hoa," replied
Fetterman.

"And I'd like to suggest that someone put a patrol out from the sugar mill," said Gerber. "A routine ambush patrol that will help us cover our movements."

"That's no problem," said Jewell. "I'll get on the horn and arrange it."

"Then we'll hit the field about three this afternoon and we'll be able to get into position by eight or nine tonight. If we stick to the swamps and the cover, they won't see us coming."

"Good."

They all walked on until they reached the perimeter. There, they stopped and stared into the distance to the west. Gerber wondered if the other men were sharing his thoughts, that their target was undoubtedly telling the villagers that the Americans and the puppet soldiers from Saigon would be there to kill them in retribution for the death of their friend, that the Americans would kill them because all Vietnamese looked the same to them. He was in for a real surprise, Gerber knew.

THROUGHOUT THE NIGHT there were sounds in the jungle around them. First there was the buzzing of insects, then the noise made by animals as they stalked or tried to avoid one another. From the distance came the boom of artillery or the rumble of bombing, including an Arc Light, which Tyme felt rather than heard. And finally there was the barely audible noise of the enemy slipping through the jungle searching for them.

Tyme had spread the men out, facing in opposite directions with their feet touching so that they could cover the whole area around them. He had told them to remain quiet, that the slightest movement or sound could be heard by the enemy and lead right back to them.

With the wounded man looked after, Tyme had settled down to wait for morning, knowing it was unlikely the enemy would find them if they were quiet. He spent the night with his eyes shifting over the ground in front of him as he tried to memorize the locations of the bushes, trees and fallen logs, all the while listening to the rustling of the leaves as the night breezes blew through the jungle. But despite the wind, the heat remained, held in by the thick cover of the trees, and with the humidity running high, it was like lying on the ground wrapped in a wet blanket. All in all, it was an uncomfortable night, with the sweat dripping and the desire for water growing.

Tyme ignored his thirst for most of the night. Once, he rolled to his side slowly, being careful not to crush any of the vegetation. Then he undid the buttons on the fly of his jungle fatigue pants. Zippers made noise, but the buttons popped open without a sound. He urinated, letting the liquid trickle out slowly and without a sound. It was a slow, irritating process, but it was better than getting killed because he couldn't take a little discomfort.

When morning finally arrived, heralded by monkeys squealing in the treetops and birds shouting the news, Tyme checked the men around him. All of them had been quiet throughout the night, probably using their fear to keep them awake. Who could sleep with snakes crawling around looking for food? Tyme hadn't told them that few snakes would hunt at night.

Slowly he extricated himself from his hiding place, moving carefully because of the stiffness of his muscles. He stood upright next to a teak tree, one hand on the smooth trunk, searching the ground in front of him. But there was no sign of the enemy. With the sun, Tyme felt better. Charlie would be in hiding now, afraid of American air power.

Tyme headed back to the wreckage of the chopper with the flight crew. As he approached, he heard a voice speaking quietly. He waved the men down, pointed to positions and used sign language to tell them to remain in place. Then he crawled forward, easing his way across the dank jungle floor, the odor of rotting vegetation and wet earth in his nostrils.

As he neared the chopper, he heard the voice again, speaking in Vietnamese. He worked his way around until he was near the base of a palm tree. From his position he could see four VC, all dressed in black pajamas. Scrambling over the chopper and pulling at the equipment left behind, they were wearing Ho Chi Minh sandals and webgear, the latter including a chest pouch that held banana clips for AKs.

Tyme searched for signs that there were more than four. They piled the stolen equipment near the cargo compartment door, seeming to take it for granted that the crew was gone and that no one would be back. There was no sign that they had posted guards.

He slipped his thumb forward along the side of his M-16 and flipped the safety to the automatic position. Then he turned the weapon slowly until the barrel was pointed in the direction of the enemy soldiers.

As he watched, they yanked something out of the cockpit and then two of them carried it to the pile. One of them held it in his hand while the other stood slightly behind him, looking over his shoulder. The man holding the device raised his voice and called to the others. They approached, and all four of them stood there talking about the object.

Tyme couldn't believe his luck—all four of them grouped together! He raised his rifle to his shoulder, put his sights on the chest of the man on the right and took a deep breath. Letting half of the air out, he pulled the trigger. The burst crashed into the stillness of the jungle. Birds flashed from their perches. Monkeys screamed in terror. There was a single shout and a cry of pain.

Tyme swung the weapon from right to left emptying the magazine. Grouped together as they had been, the four men never stood a chance.

When his weapon was empty, the bolt locked back, and Tyme dropped the magazine onto the ground. Ripping another from his bandolier, he jammed it home, worked the bolt and chambered a round. Then he waited, listening, watching.

A sudden noise behind him made him turn around. The AC loomed out of the greenish light of the jungle, his face a mask.

"What the hell?" he rasped.

Tyme shook his head and waved the man down. He then turned his attention back to the crash site. After several minutes, with the normal sounds of the jungle growing again, the buzzing of insects and the scampering of monkeys, Tyme stood up. He moved forward cautiously, his eyes on the dead men.

One of them lay on his back, his brain a visible gray-green mass. Another's shirt was a wet mess, and the ground near him was stained rusty red. Flies had begun to swarm, huge blue-black-green things that were diving into the blood. Already the face of one man was covered by them.

Tyme kept his eyes on the bodies. He listened for the sounds of others approaching as he moved closer. Before checking the dead men, he kicked their weapons away from them. He had to pry the butt of an AK from the dead fingers of one of the men. Then he tossed the weapons a few feet so that they were close to the crashed chopper.

With that accomplished, he began the grim task of checking the bodies. Each man had been riddled. The shoulders, chest and head of each had been destroyed by the M-16's bullets. It was enough to make any pathologist sick.

Tyme crouched near one of the corpses and touched the pockets. He pulled a wallet from one and some folded papers from another. Dropping them onto the ground near the body, he moved to the next. Carefully he searched each of them, tossing the documents and personal items onto the ground. When he finished, he moved back and picked up everything.

As he entered the jungle again, the AC came toward him. "You robbing the dead?"

Tyme stared at the man for a moment and then whispered, "I'm gathering intelligence. Those four men weren't just wandering the jungle and happened onto a crashed helicopter. They were enemy soldiers with some sort of a mission."

"So what did you find out?"

"They aren't VC. They're dressed like VC, but they're NVA regulars."

"How can you tell?"

Tyme shook his head, thinking that they shouldn't be holding the discussion in the jungle. They should be moving away from the site toward the open where they could signal a chopper. Quietly, patiently, he said, "Haircut, build and weapons. No insignia, but a wallet with some interesting information. Now let's get the fuck out of here.''

Before the AC could respond, Tyme pushed past him, moving toward the others. He hesitated long enough to tell them they had to get out.

"We've got to destroy the helicopter," said the Peter Pilot.

"How long?"

He shrugged. "Three minutes. Shoot a couple of holes in the fuel cells, give the JP-4 a chance to drain and then toss in a grenade."

"Or you could just open the sumps," suggested the AC, "let some fuel out and throw in the grenade. That way you don't have to make noise firing."

"Then let's do it," said Tyme.

He turned and started back to the chopper. The Peter Pilot and the AC joined him. At the site, they moved the bodies closer to the aircraft, tossed everything they couldn't carry or didn't need into the cargo compartment and then moved back. The AC opened one of the sumps, staying with it until there was a large pool of fuel under the aircraft.

"Better stand back," he warned.

Tyme and the Peter Pilot retreated into the jungle while the AC stood there measuring distances. He took a smoke grenade and pulled the pin, holding the safety spoon in place, then kept moving back until he was near a large tree. Finally he tossed the grenade. It rolled under the chopper, billowing bright yellow. The flame from it ignited the JP-4, which began to burn furiously. The fire spread rapidly.

Tyme had wanted to watch, but the fire was burning too fast and too hot. He was afraid of an explosion. Grabbing the AC by the shoulder, he jerked him to the rear.

"Let's get out of here."

The AC looked at Tyme, then at the aircraft. "Yeah. Let's git."

They began to run through the jungle. Behind them was the sound of the aircraft burning. There were quiet pops and bangs as the magnesium ignited and then a rocking explosion as the fuel cells went up. Tyme was convinced he felt a hot wind from the detonation roll up his back.

At the camp Tyme stopped and turned. He was too far from the burning wreckage to see anything—the jungle was too dense—but he thought he could smell it. "That'll bring them from all over."

"It'll bring in our people, too," said the AC.

"Then we'd better get out into the open where we can be spotted."

"How do we do that?"

"Spread a panel and throw out some smoke when an aircraft is near. They'll investigate, and if we can convince them we're Americans, they'll be in to pick us up."

"Yeah," agreed the AC. "Shouldn't be too hard."

Unless there are VC around, thought Tyme.

SANTINI SAT IN THE TEAM HOUSE, eating a late breakfast of cold cereal and warm orange juice. He didn't like Rice Krispies, but it was all that had been left. For variety, he had sliced a banana into them, poured on the milk that he had made from powder and water and begun to eat. It wasn't the best breakfast he had ever eaten, but at least it wasn't costing him anything.

The team house was a replica of all the others he had seen during his tour in Vietnam. A small structure, partially underground to protect it from mortar attacks, it was loaded with tables and chairs like a restaurant and had a refrigerator in one corner and a large tub holding water and a block of ice in another. About a third of the room was blocked by a waist-high counter that separated the cooking facilities from the dining room. There was an old stove, a sink and shelves full of canned goods.

Just as Santini finished his breakfast, the team commander, Captain Richard Bundt, entered. Bundt was a tall man who had first learned of the Special Forces in Bad Tolz, Germany, when he had engaged in a fight with several Green Berets. He had thought the green hats they wore were funny. He had lost the fight eventually, and they had suggested that

PULL THE PIN
ON ADVENTURE,

....get 4 explosive novels plus a pocketknife
FREE

Score a direct hit by accepting our dynamite free offer

Here's a no-holds-barred, free-for-all chance for you to blast your way through the hottest action-adventure novels ever published.

Just return the attached card, and we'll send you 4 gut-chilling, high-voltage novels just like the one you're reading— plus a versatile pocketknife— ABSOLUTELY FREE!

They're yours to keep even if you never buy another Gold Eagle novel. But we're betting you'll want to join the legion of fans who get Gold Eagle books delivered right to their home on a regular basis. Here's why...

7 GREAT REASONS TO BECOME A SUBSCRIBER:

As a Gold Eagle subscriber, you'll get: • 6 new titles every other month • 11% savings off retail prices—you pay only $2.49 per book plus 95¢ postage and handling per shipment • books hot off the presses and before they're available at retail stores • delivery right to your home • FREE newsletter with every shipment • always the right to cancel and owe nothing • eligibility to receive special books at deep discount prices

The grenade's in your hand. Go for it!

This offer is too good to miss...
RUSH YOUR ORDER TO US TODAY

he join their outfit. Now, fifteen years later, he was commanding an A-Detachment in Vietnam.

Bundt poured himself a cup of coffee and sat down opposite Santini. In English that carried only the slightest trace of an accent, he asked, "You have to go out this morning?"

Santini dropped his spoon into the empty cereal bowl. "I'd have to call Nha Trang and tell Major Madden I've been held up, but no, I don't have to return this morning. What's the problem?"

Bundt waved a hand at the empty space behind the counter where a Vietnamese woman would normally be working. "Viets didn't come in this morning."

"What do you mean?"

Bundt leaned forward, his elbows on the table. "I mean, since there's a town right outside, we hire laborers from the local population. Seventy-five people come in daily to take care of the chores, cooking, cleaning, shining our boots, burning the shit, all that sort of thing. Only none of them came in this morning."

"Christ, Captain," said Santini. "That would mean..."

"Yeah. Something's up. We've had an indication of it for the past few days—men from the strike companies reporting things to us. But this is the first tangible thing. Might just mean a mortar attack, or it could be something more serious."

"So what's the plan?"

Now Bundt smiled. "Well, if we can count on your help, there are a number of things I want to do."

"As I said, I'll need to coordinate with my boss in Nha Trang, but I think I'll be able to stay." Santini picked up his juice and finished it. He set the glass down carefully, as if afraid it would break.

"Good. You take charge of the prisoners. Watch them closely if we get into any kind of fight. That'll leave my men to take care of the jobs they've been assigned."

Santini pushed his bowl away and leaned forward. "That's not much of a task."

"On the surface, no. But if the enemy hits the wire, it could become very important. And if we're in danger of being overrun, having one more American in the camp will be that much more help. Right now, if you take charge of the prisoners, it'll be the best thing for us."

"I'll be happy to help out, sir."

Bundt stood. "Good. Very good. I'll see you after you coordinate with Nha Trang."

As Bundt left, Santini wondered what he had gotten himself into.

10

HIEP HOA, SOUTH VIETNAM

It was a short chopper flight from Duc Hoa to Hiep Hoa. The aircraft landed on the short red dirt runway at Duc Hoa near the large pond and sat with its rotors spinning. Gerber, Fetterman, Albright and two Vietnamese strikers moved to it in a slow run, ducking their heads as if they believed the rotors would suddenly flex and lop them off.

They leaped up into the cargo compartment. The crew chief looked around from his well, saw that they were all seated and then rocked back. The chopper lifted up in a swirling, dense cloud of dirt and began to race along the runway, leaving the dirt and whirling debris behind it.

They climbed rapidly and then broke to the northwest. Below them was the shimmering shape of the Oriental River, known as the Song Vam Co Dong. An expanse of light green sparkled in the afternoon sun, marking the Plain of Reeds. They stayed close to the river. Gerber saw sampans littering the bank. It appeared as if the occupants had heard the chopper and rowed ashore, abandoning their boats so that the Americans wouldn't shoot them. There were dozens of little tributaries off the river, many of them weed-choked and partially overgrown. The scattered bush and tough grasses would make travel through the swamp difficult but not impossible.

It was exactly the terrain everyone would avoid, which made it perfect.

To the east was another swamp, but there was more dry ground in it. Large clumps of trees hid farmers' hootches—three or four hootches to a cluster, with water buffalo pens and family bunkers. There were people in the fields, working without looking up, except for the young men who stared defiantly into the sky. Gerber expected them to flip him the finger, but they only stared, their faces glistening with sweat and hate.

The chopper turned east then, just south of the sugar mill, which was a wall-enclosed plant. Gerber suspected that at one time it had actually been a sugar mill, but as far as he knew no sugar was being processed there now. They came up on the camp at Hiep Hoa and crossed at altitude. Suddenly the chopper rolled onto its side and dived toward the ground, its nose pointed at the center of the camp. Gerber grabbed the edge of the troop seat, figuring that the pilot had suddenly gone insane. At the last possible instant, the helicopter leveled out and the nose rose. They seemed to be lying on their backs, the snout of the aircraft pointing straight up. The forward motion was arrested, and as the nose dropped and the aircraft started to settle, the pilot sucked in pitch. The touchdown was so gentle that Gerber wasn't sure the skids were on the ground.

As soon as they made ground contact, Fetterman and Albright leaped out. The Vietnamese followed and then Gerber. Almost before his feet hit the dirt, the chopper lifted and began a racing takeoff, climbing into the sky rapidly.

They all stood there for a moment, dumbfounded, until a short, stocky man with black hair and a sunburned face came up to them. He was wearing sweat-damp fatigues, a pistol belt that held a single canteen and a .45 automatic, and jungle boots. His beret was molded to his head, and his captain's bars, pinned to the flash, caught the sunlight and reflected it.

He came close but didn't hold out his hand to be shaken, and no one saluted. He stood there for a moment. "You're the special team?"

"That we are," said Gerber.

"You can wait in the team house for dark, if that's what you want, or I can show you the way out."

Gerber checked his watch. "We'd like to rest in the team house for an hour or so. We don't want to leave too early."

"Fine." He turned to go and then spun, grinning. "Sorry. Name's Hampton. Figured you boys wouldn't be here very long and didn't see the point in talking about it."

Gerber raised his eyebrows. "Whatever."

"Like I said, I didn't mean to be rude. Figured the less I knew about this, the better off I'd be."

"I understand." Gerber watched the men shoulder their equipment, then followed Hampton as he walked deeper into his camp. It looked just like a hundred other camps: buildings that looked half-finished with screens in the upper levels and tin roofs, surrounded by four-foot-high sandbag walls. Inside a couple, Gerber saw cots with sweating men lying on them.

They passed between several buildings and entered a redoubt, an earthwork wall about five feet high. There were a few buildings in it. One was obviously a dispensary because of the red cross on it. Hampton took them into the team house and told them to make themselves comfortable.

As they sat down, he asked, "How long you boys going to be here?"

"Give us an hour."

"You want something to drink, you ask My Tran, and she'll rustle it up for you. I'll be back in about an hour."

When Hampton was gone, Fetterman got a glass of ice water. He was tempted to get iced tea, but he only drank it with sugar, and the last thing he wanted was something with sugar in it. He returned to the table, sat down and asked, "Now what?"

Gerber shrugged. "Now we wait. Then we move into the field." He pulled his map out of his pocket and opened it carefully on the table, smoothing out the creases. Then he began to study it.

Fetterman slid his chair around so that he could see it also and Albright came over to stand behind them. They had done it all at Duc Hoa, but Gerber liked to be familiar with an area before he moved into it. The problem here was that there weren't any landmarks, just lots of open, swampy ground and rice paddies with villages and hamlets near them, some so small they had no names. Others were so temporary they moved with the changing seasons. A mud hootch could be put up quickly and would literally melt in the monsoon without someone there to repair it.

Albright left them, got a glass of water and returned. He looked at the Vietnamese woman, a pleasant-looking girl of twenty who dressed in the style of the Americans. She wore a blouse and a skirt and wore her long hair straight. Though she smiled at them frequently, she kept her distance.

"There's not much there," said Albright, pointing. He kept his eyes on the girl.

"We'll just have to be careful," said Gerber. He finally picked up the map and put it away. Then he picked up his weapon and began to check it again. Fetterman followed the lead.

In almost no time Hampton was back. "If you're ready?"

Gerber stood, shouldered his pack and nodded. The pack didn't contain much because they would be operating close to their base and didn't plan to be out long. There were C-rations in the pack, the crummy stuff such as the canned bread and the ham and lima beans weeded out and given to the Vietnamese. He had clean, dry socks and extra ammo. He had two spare batteries for the URC-10 radio because he knew the trouble they could have in the swamp if they needed to make radio contact with anyone. And he had a flashlight, along with his first-aid kit, bug repellant that he was reluctant to use and his toothbrush.

Wiggling his shoulders, he got the rucksack seated properly, folded his beret and stuck it inside. As he donned an OD green baseball cap and nodded, he saw that the other team members were ready, too.

Hampton escorted them to the flimsy gate and opened it. He held out a hand. "Good luck."

Albright and one of the Vietnamese headed down the dirt road that led to the short runway. They traversed it, their feet stirring up little clouds of dust in the hot afternoon sun, then entered a field of elephant grass. They seemed to descend, as if walking down a ramp, until only their heads and shoulders were visible.

Great place for the enemy to form for an attack, Gerber thought, but as he followed he realized it wasn't all that great. The ground was soft and spongy, and they quickly left the elephant grass. The water from the swamp was at first only ankle-deep and then knee-deep and finally waist-deep. Gerber had thought walking through the swamp would be a cool proposition, but the water was tepid and the exertion made him sweat. Within a hundred yards he was breathing as if he had run a kilometer. His mouth was dry and the sweat stained his face, dripping from his forehead and stinging his eyes.

He reached down to splash some of the water onto his face and caught a whiff of it. There was a foul stench to the water as if something had died in it. The whole swamp stunk like an open sewer, and Gerber felt his stomach turn over at the thought of walking through it.

At first they moved south from Hiep Hoa, figuring that any Vietcong in the local strike companies would be interested in their movements. As soon as they were out of sight of Hiep Hoa, hidden from the camp by the elephant grass and the lay of the land, they turned north. Eventually they came to a tree line and climbed out of the water. Once inside the clump of trees, they spread out for a quick rest. Gerber checked his weapon again, making sure he had kept the barrel out of the water.

Spread out like a carpet around them was the swamp, punctuated here and there with a few tree lines that reached out like giant fingers trying to pull the carpeting out from under them. Gerber moved through the trees and looked out the other side.

Fetterman approached and said, "You know, Captain, if we follow this, it'll provide us with cover and won't take us that far away from our target. After dark we'll be able to slip into place."

"Albright say he can find his way in the dark?"

"He seemed to think it would be no problem."

"Then I can't see any reason we should continue cross-country. We'll stay in the shade."

"Take us a little longer to get into position," said Fetterman.

"But we'll stay out of sight better."

Gerber checked the time again, then signaled Albright. The Special Forces NCO got to his feet, checked his compass and began moving through the trees.

The tree line wasn't like the triple-canopy jungle they sometimes had to walk through; it was more like a well-kept park, with only sparse vegetation that grabbed and clung. But the undergrowth could easily be avoided, since it was only short grass and prickly bush. With the shade provided by the overhanging branches, the sun was kept off them. The air was still hot and humid, but they didn't have the sun frying them.

Albright picked up the pace, moving around the trees, trying to stay close to the center of the tree line. They found evidence of other American patrols—tin cans covered with fungus that grew on the scraps left in them; a couple of rounds of ammo, the brass tarnished jade green, suggesting they'd been there for a while; a bit of rotting cloth; and inexplicably, one boot, the leather beginning to disintegrate. They ignored it all, moving on.

Late in the afternoon they came to the end of the tree line. Albright halted them at the very edge of it, where they could look out at the swamp, beyond which was slightly higher ground, some of it divided into rice paddies. A few farmers still worked their fields. All were dressed in black shorts and coolie hats, and none of them looked up as aircraft passed overhead.

Gerber circulated, telling Fetterman and the two Vietnamese to relax for a few minutes. He instructed them to eat and drink something. After they had done that, the guard would be rotated so that Gerber and Albright could do the same.

WITH TYME IN THE LEAD, they moved through the jungle slowly. The two in the middle carried a stretcher made from a poncho liner and a couple of saplings. They worked their way through the thick vegetation, being careful not to leave any signs. Tyme enforced noise discipline and walked the point, signaling the men to tell them of booby traps, pitfalls and the clinging vines that would tear at their clothes. He kept the pace steady, stopping every hour to rest for ten minutes.

Tyme was accustomed to the heat and humidity, but the flight crew wasn't. In the first few moments they were soaked with sweat, breathing through their mouths and moving increasingly slower. They also took more frequent turns carrying the wounded man.

At a large clearing, Tyme held up a hand and waved the flight crew into hiding. He then crouched, leaned his left shoulder against a tree trunk and studied the clearing. It was forty or fifty yards long and the same in width. Scrub brush and short grass covered it, and there were a number of saplings scattered throughout.

Tyme shifted around. There was nothing on the ground near him. No sign of bunkers or enemy camps. In the jungle, where the LZs were rare, the enemy sometimes ringed them with bunkers. The bunkers weren't always manned, but none were visible here.

Lifting a hand, Tyme wiped his face, rubbing the sweat onto his fatigue jacket as he listened to the birdcalls. Overhead a bright green bird wheeled in the air and then dived for the treetops opposite him. Then there was a rustling, and Tyme saw the thick body of a brightly colored snake as it disappeared into a bush ten feet away. Since the snake wasn't coming toward him, Tyme ignored it. Instead, he peered through the drooping branches of a broad-leaved giant fern, waiting for someone to show himself.

After thirty minutes, Tyme was convinced there was no one around the clearing. He noticed that the flight crewmen had concealed themselves among the short grass and brightly flowered bushes near the bases of the tall jungle trees. They hadn't done a good job of it, but at least they had tried, and he hadn't heard their movement. He motioned for them to remain in place, then slipped out of hiding. Skirting the edge of the jungle, staying only in the shadows, he moved north. The ground was soft and the grass dusty. It was an even coat, suggesting that no one had been around recently. When he was satisfied there was no trap waiting to be sprung, he stopped again.

Using a poncho liner, Tyme folded it into an oblong panel and set it in the center of the clearing. He worked rapidly, the heat of the sun baking him. In seconds he was sweating heavily and breathing hard. The strain of walking through the jungle was almost nothing compared to working in the sun.

With the panel set, he retreated to the cover of the vegetation. He took out a red smoke grenade and placed it near his foot. Then, with one hand on the ground he crouched, waiting for an enemy patrol. Try as he might, he couldn't shake the feeling that they were in the jungle around him somewhere, even though he hadn't seen any sign of them.

He listened for the welcome pop of rotor blades, signaling the presence of a helicopter. If one came close, he would throw the smoke. Seeing it, the pilot would veer toward the clearing and spot the panel. He probably wouldn't land, but he would investigate, and that would lead to their rescue.

It was quiet for almost an hour, with no sound other than the animals, birds and the high-flying jets. Then, in the distance, he heard the approaching chopper. He reached down and picked up the grenade. As the sound came closer, he moved to the edge of the clearing. When it was obvious that the chopper was going to cross the clearing, he pulled the pin and tossed the grenade into the center of the LZ.

For a heart-stopping instant it seemed to Tyme that no one on the aircraft had seen anything. Then the chopper banked left and came around. Tyme stepped into the sunlight, moving toward the panel. He took off his beret and waved it, then saw the crew chief lean out and wave back.

The helicopter broke away, disappearing from sight, but Tyme could still hear it. When the sound started to get louder again, Tyme retreated into the jungle. He moved rapidly toward the downed flyers and rasped, "Let's move it."

He didn't think the helicopter would land, but in case it did, he didn't want it sitting on the ground for very long.

The others scrambled from cover, two of them lifting the makeshift stretcher. They hurried forward, and Tyme waved them back to cover at the very edge of the LZ.

The helicopter swooped down as Tyme crouched at the edge of the clearing. The skids almost brushed the leaves off the tallest trees. It flared suddenly, and the noise from the engine increased as the blades popped. The grass was flattened as if a hurricane had suddenly hit. Loose grass, leaves, twigs and the smoke from the still-billowing grenade swirled around as they were sucked up by the chopper.

Tyme rushed out, his hands held high, his weapon over his head. The door gunner, sitting behind his M-60, tracked Tyme until he was sure that he was an American. As the others emerged from the darkness of the jungle, the door gunner followed them the same way. Then all of them were climbing into the chopper or helping to lift the stretcher in. When the last man stepped up onto the skids, Tyme held a thumb up and nodded. The AC didn't need any encouragement. He pulled in the pitch, and the chopper leaped into the air.

When they crossed the tree line, and the clearing was no longer visible, Tyme breathed a sigh of relief. They were safe for the moment.

The crew chief worked his way out of his well, touched Tyme on the shoulder and shouted, "Who are you guys?"

As soon as Tyme explained it, the crew chief let out a rebel yell and said, "Welcome back to the world of the living."

THEY PASSED AN HOUR RESTING. The sun changed from a glowing yellow ball to an orange blob as it dropped toward the ground. Soon the rice paddies and the farmers' hootches were wrapped in purple shadows. The sound of Vietnamese music drifted on a light breeze, not AFVN but a Saigon station. Lights suddenly appeared and flickered as lanterns and fires were lit.

Gerber ate his cold meal, drank his warm water and then leaned against the trunk of a tall tree. He closed his eyes for a moment and tried to isolate the sounds around him. Insects buzzed, a water buffalo bellowed and several unidentifiable animals screeched. Then there was a sharp burst of Vietnamese as a wife yelled at her husband.

Soon the ground around him began to darken and disappear. The definition of the bushes and trees faded and blended until it was a single black mass full of scrambling tiny claws and the calls of frightened animals. When it was completely dark, with only the sounds of the breeze through the trees and a distant radio, Gerber got to his feet and moved forward. He touched Fetterman on the shoulder and leaned close to the master sergeant's ear.

"Think it's time?"

Fetterman nodded, then realized Gerber wouldn't be able to see the gesture in the dark. "Yes, sir," he whispered. He slid to the rear and stood slowly, the bones of his knees popping like corks from wine bottles.

Without another word, the small patrol formed, with Albright in the lead and one of the Vietnamese strikers beside him. The sergeant stepped off to avoid the razorlike leaves of a bush, staying just inside the tree line. His gaze remained on the gray expanse of rice paddies and open fields just beyond the trees. Then he turned north and crouched for a moment before slipping out of cover. He stepped on a rice paddy dike, then eased his way down its steep slope so that he was standing ankle-deep in the foul-smelling water. Moving along there, he rolled his foot from heel to toe to keep the mud from making a sucking sound.

The men of the patrol strung out behind him, dropping farther apart as they left the protection of the tree line. They moved across the rice fields in a low crouch until they came to a clump of trees with a half-dozen hootches hidden among the tall palms. A single light burned with the whiteness of a lantern, and there was quiet music from a Vietnamese station.

The patrol kept moving across more rice paddies that finally gave way to more swamp. Gerber didn't like moving through the swamp at night, but that couldn't be helped. At first it was only knee-deep, but they were soon up to their chests. The tall grasses and reeds covered their movements, and the wind from the west covered their sound.

As they worked their way deeper toward their target, Gerber kept his eyes on the stars blazing overhead. Somehow they seemed brighter than those above the cold November swamps of North Carolina only a few weeks before.

The air was also filled with the sound of jet aircraft and propeller-driven fighter planes. When those came close, the patrol halted and crouched, the water up to their necks, and when the planes passed, they began moving again.

After nearly an hour in the swamp, they came to a short rise topped by a road. They fanned out along it, but there was no traffic. Albright took a compass reading and then climbed from the swamp and slipped across the road on his belly. When he was in the water on the other side, the rest of the patrol followed him one at a time.

They made their way through the tepid water for another half hour, then Albright stopped. He held a hand up briefly, then moved toward a small island in the middle of the swamp. The land was dry and covered with thick grass and short bushes. He crawled up on it and then returned to Gerber.

"We've arrived. Good cover here."

Gerber followed him back to the island. In the distance he could see a two-story building, yellow light burning in two of the windows.

"That it?"

"Yeah."

Gerber took out his binoculars and studied it closely. In the dark it was hard to see anything except the rusting tin of the roof and the pale color of the walls. There were dark words painted on one side in Vietnamese. Music drifted on the breeze.

Gerber leaned close to Albright. "That what I think it is?"

"If you think it's a bordello, then it's what you think it is."

"Shit!" said Gerber. He tucked his binoculars into his pack. "That explains why they can get away with showing light like that."

Fetterman slipped up on them and whispered, "There's a clump of trees on dry ground about a hundred yards to the west. It'll put us about fifty yards from the rear of the house."

Gerber turned and peered into the darkness until he discerned the darker shapes of the trees. "You take one of the strikers and a radio and cover it."

"Just one thing. How are we going to know if our boy is in there?" asked Fetterman.

"Albright?"

"Let Nguyen walk in and take a look around," said Albright.

"Or we could just stake out the place and watch for our guy," Fetterman suggested. "If he arrives later, we're in good shape. If he's there already, it means we'll have to spend another day out here."

Gerber shook his head, thinking rapidly. It was the one problem with the plan. They had to either stake out the house and wait patiently or send in someone to look. The safest bet was to hang back and scrutinize everyone as he entered.

"Won't Nguyen be recognized?"

"No. He should be okay," said Albright.

Gerber was about to give permission and then realized that patience was its own virtue. "No," he said. "We keep our eyes open, and if we see him go in, then we move. If we don't, we'll lie low during the day."

"Sir—"

"That's it, Sergeant," said Gerber.

"Yes, sir."

"If our man doesn't show up by an hour before dawn, I want everyone to go to ground. We cover ourselves and play possum until tomorrow night. Questions?"

"Sir, if he sneaks in the back, you might not see him, though I would," said Fetterman.

"Then you get a message to us. Radio checks on five after the hour. If he shows, we'll make the strike about three in the morning. That's when everyone should be at the lowest ebb."

"Yes, sir."

"Then let's get at it."

Fetterman touched the shoulder of one of the strikers and slipped into the swamp. There was quiet splashing and then silence.

Gerber crawled forward until he was at the lip of the island, the water inches from his face. Again he dug out his binoculars and studied the front of the building. There was a covered porch with flickering candlelight and shapes were moving. More light filtered from a window, illuminating a Vietnamese woman in a skirt but no blouse.

Albright whispered, "If he comes, it'll be in a car. He's an important man and has a car. That's how we'll know for sure. And I don't see a car out there now."

"Good," said Gerber. "There's a chance we'll get him tonight."

"Could we get that lucky?"

"Sure," said Gerber, not believing it.

11

SONG BE SPECIAL
FORCES CAMP

It was midmorning before Tyme was able to get back to Song
Be. He had been forced to spend the night at Tay Ninh after
the rescue. By the time all the debriefings had been attended
and all the intelligence obtained, Tyme couldn't get a flight
back to Song Be. He had wanted to share his observations with
Captain Bromhead, to tell the captain that he thought the enemy was beginning to swarm into their AO.

On the flight back to Song Be, Tyme had thought about the
word. Swarm was the right one. Just as bees when the hive
became too crowded and they swarmed to find a new place of
residence, it seemed that the enemy was out searching. He
hadn't seen that many of them, it was true, but coupled with
everything else, including the fact the VC felt confident
enough to fire on the chopper in daylight, something seemed
to be in the air.

They landed on the red dirt runway, and Tyme was surprised that no one was out there to meet him. The helicopter
took off as soon as Tyme had climbed out. He stood there for
a moment, looking to the east where the Montagnards had
their village. Then he turned and looked at the star-shaped
camp. Beyond it, far to the west, he could see black clouds
boiling, but the rain was falling into the jungle.

He waited for a jeep from the compound, but nothing came for him. Finally he shouldered his weapon and began the short walk into the camp. He was a little upset that they weren't out there to welcome him home, especially after all he had been through, but then it was another workday and he hadn't told them what time he would return, only that it would be sometime in the morning.

Using the wide road, he walked between the wires and entered through the camp's wooden gate. It was strangely quiet in the compound. There had been a flicker of movement behind the firing ports of some of the bunkers, but that would be the men on guard. The compound itself was deserted.

Tyme was going to head to his hootch and drop off his gear, but then decided he should tell Bromhead that he was back. He detoured toward the team house, wondering if he was walking into a trap. The thought came to him that the camp might have been overrun in the night and the enemy was now letting him walk in. The thought wasn't as crazy as it sounded because the old Triple Nickel had been taken by the enemy. Of course there had been evidence then—burned buildings and wrecked helicopters.

Before he reached the team house, the door burst open. Grenades flew out and hit the ground near his feet. Tyme stood still as each of the grenades popped, then began to billow Technicolor clouds of smoke. He was wrapped in it, losing sight of the team house, the compound and the sky. He smelled the burnt gunpowder, which reminded him of Fourth of July displays when he was a kid.

Then there was a shout—a single voice that was quickly joined by others who penetrated the cloud. Tyme was surrounded by his friends, who shouted, laughed and slapped him on the back.

"Welcome home!" yelled Bromhead.

"Good to see you," said Bocker, taking the weapon from Tyme. He was going to tell Tyme that he had been out searching for him, and that he had been recalled when the chopper had picked Tyme out of the jungle, but the moment passed.

The others crowded around him, shaking his hand and asking questions so fast that he couldn't answer them. As the cloud of colored smoke began to dissipate and the sun was visible again, Bromhead eased Tyme toward the team house. "Come and tell us about your adventures."

"Not much to tell."

"There's enough," said the young captain. "The aviation boys have put you in for a medal."

They entered the team house, and Tyme collapsed into a chair. He glanced at the familiar surroundings and felt an excitement surge through him, a gladness to be home after the ordeal in the jungle. He clapped his hands together and laughed.

"Bring him a beer," ordered Bromhead.

One of the sergeants spun and jerked open the refrigerator. He grabbed a beer and tossed it toward Tyme, who caught it one-handed. After opening the can and taking a long drink, Tyme said, "Yeah. That's what I needed."

"Now tell us what happened," said Bromhead.

"First, I think I better get with Sergeant Yeakly so that he can pass my observations on to Nha Trang."

"And those are?" asked Bromhead.

"That something big is going to happen in the next few days. Something very big."

MORROW SAT AT HER DESK reading the latest news reports from Khe Sanh. Communist forces were scattered in the hills around the base and had been lobbing mortar, rocket and artillery rounds into the camp almost without letup. The press corps was trying to get in to look around, but the military was suggesting it was too dangerous. There were reports that a siege was shaping up and that the Communists were viewing it as another Dien Bien Phu—one great victory over the Americans to force them out of the country.

Morrow read through the reports twice and decided they were just a lot of hype. It seemed to her that each reporter in the area was trying to convince his boss that he was on top of the biggest story of the war. Morrow slowly wadded the paper into a giant ball and threw it at the wastebasket.

"What bullshit," she said.

Marvin Crown, a young man on his first overseas assignment, picked up the paper and dropped it into the can. A short, slim man with light hair and almost nonexistent eyebrows, he moved to her desk and asked, "What's bullshit?"

"This whole thing," she said, waving a hand that could have taken in the newsroom, Saigon or all of South Vietnam.

Crown grabbed a vacant chair and pulled it close. As he sat down, he asked, "Why do you say that?"

"Because everyone is looking at his own story and refusing to see the big picture. Something is going to happen. The military knows it, but we ignore it. We're too caught up in our own stories and our own reporting to see it."

"If you're so sure of that," said Crown, "then why are you sitting here bitching about it? Why aren't you out looking for the proof of what you say?"

"Because it's all going to happen here and I don't have to worry about it." But even as she said it, she realized how lame it sounded. She was just going to sit on her hands and wait for the story to come to her. That wasn't good journalism. It was what historians did—visit the hills after the battle to talk about it. But she should be in the hills reporting it as it happened.

There were a dozen things that she should do, a hundred people she should interview. There were stories to be written, and if Hodges and the editors wouldn't approve them now, they certainly would in a week when the enemy came swarming up the streets shooting at everyone. She should get over to MACV and talk to the generals and colonels who now had the time to talk. She would be able to lead the discussions because no one else would be interested in it. When the enemy appeared, the generals and colonels would be too busy to talk to reporters. They would be fighting the battle they were preparing for.

Morrow stood and shouldered her camera bag. "Thanks, Marv. I needed that."

"What'd I do?"

"You got me off my butt and out into the field."

Now he stood, too, and put a hand on her forearm. "Hey, if you've got something cooking, you should share it with me. I need a story, too."

Morrow was going to try to shake him, then she realized the story was going to be bigger than she could handle. It would be bigger than the entire staff could handle when it finally broke.

"Grab your tape recorder and let's go see what we can find out."

"Yeah!" said Crown, excited. "Yeah. Let's go."

GERBER LAY QUIETLY under the protective branches of a large bush, the fragrance of its yellow flowers overpowering. The ground under him wasn't dry. It was a spongy, damp, rotting mess that was slowly seeping through his uniform. He was wet on one side because of the swamp and damp on the other because of the sun. He was sweating heavily and breathing through his mouth like a panting dog. He hadn't realized that lying on the ground could be such hard work.

Throughout the morning he had used his binoculars to study the hootch in front of him. In his mind he thought of it as a hootch, just one more Vietnamese structure, but somehow this building belied his definition. Could a two-story house, with shutters at the windows, a balcony on the second floor with French doors opening onto it from any of four rooms, be called a hootch? It was a mini-hotel that had been turned into a brothel, which conducted a thriving business from both sides.

It was a strange thing to see. Earlier that morning there had been an American on the balcony—a pale, fat man with a beachball stomach over his OD green shorts. The man's arms were deeply tanned, as was his face, but the rest of him was pasty white. He had stood in the morning sun, one hand on the railing of the balcony and one hand on his massive belly. After a few moments, a tiny Vietnamese girl wearing nothing at all had joined him. She had rubbed herself against him and tried to tug him back into the room. The man had resisted for several seconds and then turned to follow her.

There seemed to be some kind of unofficial neutrality about the house. Both sides used it and each side ignored the other. The VC and NVA and the Americans and South Vietnamese relieved their tensions in the house without worrying about one another. It wasn't unlike the situation at Vung Tau. Both sides used it as a recreational facility and neither attacked it.

Gerber glanced at Albright, who was lying on the other side of the bush with his head on his hands, almost as if he was asleep. Gerber whispered, "What do you know about this place?"

Albright lifted his head and looked at Gerber. "Only that it's a whorehouse and has been there for twenty years or more."

"You ever been in it?"

"You kidding? I wouldn't go near the place with a bazooka. Who knows what you'd catch there? Hell, the girls in Saigon are bad enough, and they've got to pass a few health inspections, but out here, who cares?"

"There was an American in there."

"I'm not all that surprised. Some of those guys from Cu Chi and the other big bases have no idea what's going on out here. Christ, what a way to fight a war."

Gerber nodded and turned his attention back to the house. A woman stepped out onto the porch, fanning herself. She pulled her sweat-soaked blouse away from her body and blew down the front. Then she dropped into a chair and threw her head back as if trying to catch a breeze, but there was none.

Men came and went. Some of them wore black pajamas and could have been local farmers and their sons, but somehow Gerber didn't think so. He saw a jeep pull up and four Americans, two white and two black, leap out. They scrambled up the steps, and Gerber could hear their shouts and laughter drifting out over the swamp.

At noon he put down his binoculars and drank some of his water. Slowly he ate the boned chicken from his C-rations, salting it heavily. He wished he had brought salt tablets, but hadn't expected the enforced inactivity; he had thought they would be in and out quickly. As he ate, he wondered how Fet-

terman was making out. Occasionally he had scanned the rise
where the master sergeant was hidden, but had seen nothing
there. Fetterman had done an excellent job of concealing
himself.

The heat of midafternoon brought more traffic. An army
truck full of South Vietnamese roared up and the men leaped
out over the sides in their enthusiasm. The girls rushed out
onto the balcony, shouting down at the soldiers. There was a
lot of noise and gaiety.

And even with the South Vietnamese army truck parked in
front of the place, the men in the black pajamas kept coming.
Some of them sneaked in the back while others used the front.

The whole thing amazed and amused Gerber. The war had
ceased to exist in that one tiny piece of South Vietnam. Un-
written rules were obeyed by everyone. The weapons had been
left outside and no one stole them. The men in the black pajamas sometimes looked into the truck at the scattered M-16s
and M-14s and the spare ammo, but they didn't take anything. It was a very delicate balance, and Gerber knew they
were going to upset it soon.

AS SOON AS HIS SHIFT was over, Lockridge ran to his quarters
and changed into civilian clothes. Jones wasn't far behind, and
together they left the embassy grounds, heading for the café
across the street. Lockridge believed that Le Tran would be
waiting there for him. They entered the small café, searched
the occupants and then took a table close to the front window
so that they could watch the pedestrians circulate outside.

Lockridge ordered tea and sat there sipping it. He let his
eyes wander from the scarred tabletop to the ceiling fan that
spun slowly above him. He stared into the faces of the Vietnamese customers and at the few Americans who came in. Le
Tran didn't show.

He wasn't worried because he remembered the night he'd
spent with her—the promise of things to come, her responses
to his searching hands, her moans at the touch of his probing
fingers. She had been as excited about it as he had been and
was now.

Jones looked at his watch and the deepening shadows on the sidewalk outside. "I don't think they're coming tonight."

"They'll be here," said Lockridge.

"Well, they're already over an hour late, and given the constraints of this society with its curfew and all, you'd think they'd be on time."

"Women keep you waiting," protested Lockridge. "It's their nature to keep you guessing."

Jones shook his head as he looked at his watch again. "They're not coming, I tell you."

"Then it's their parents stopping them. Won't let them out alone. We should go over to their house."

Jones raised his eyebrows. "You think you can find it?"

Now Lockridge grinned. "Of course. I was ready for something like this and kept my eyes open. I can find it again."

"Okay," said Jones, standing. He tossed a couple of bills onto the table. "Let's go."

Outside they hailed a cab, this one a Chevy that looked like a Chevy and had only a single color, a deep high-polished brown. Lockridge wondered where the driver had stolen it, but he climbed into the back seat anyway.

"You speak English?"

"A little."

"Fine. You just follow my directions and we'll all get along well."

They took off through the Saigon traffic, rocketing around the slower cars and between the giant military trucks. They nearly collided with a jeep, swerved and then almost hit a Lambretta. The driver let fly with a stream of Vietnamese that didn't wish anyone a happy new year. They roared up palm-lined streets and then down narrow ones lined with bars blaring all kinds of music. They left the city proper and entered the outskirts where the houses were old and ornate or dilapidated and new. Wires were hung from telephone poles and dead palm trees.

Lockridge got lost once, each block looking like the one they had just been on, but then he saw a small park with a tiny pond and knew that they were getting close. He ordered the driver to slow as he stared at each building, looking for the house where Le Tran had taken them.

He saw dozens of poor people who had fled the war in the countryside and were now seeking refuge in the city where they could earn a few piasters hustling. There were men missing arms and legs or both demanding money, men who wore pieces of their ARVN uniforms to prove they were honest soldiers who had served and who now needed help. And there were women in black pajamas, *ao dai* or Western-style skirts and blouses who smiled at the cab with blackened, broken teeth and offered a good time while other women claimed their sisters were virgins for the right man. And along with the men and women there were children, hundreds of them, some of them naked, running up and down the streets chasing puppies or chickens or Americans who ventured into the area.

Finally Lockridge spotted the house—a two-story structure with plywood fastened over part of the front bay window. "Stop!" he demanded. And when the driver braked, Lockridge threw open the door and leaped to the dirt path that served as a sidewalk.

"You pay now!" yelled the driver.

Lockridge stopped and whirled. "You wait right here. We pay in a few minutes. You drive us back to town."

"You pay now!"

"You wait or you don't get paid."

Apparently the driver saw the wisdom of that because he fell into a sullen silence. He beat his hand against the steering wheel, but didn't speak.

Lockridge rushed up onto the porch. He glanced over his shoulder as Jones approached. Lockridge reached up and tapped on the door, and when no one answered it he knocked harder. When that failed to get a response, Lockridge hammered on the door. It rattled in the frame and then swung open.

Lockridge stuck his head in and yelled, "Le Tran?" When he got no answer, he stepped in and called again. To the right, he saw the living room, but now it seemed to be abandoned. Some of the furniture was still there, but the record player and the records had been taken. Lockridge turned and shrugged. "I don't get it."

Jones checked the other side and then ran up the stairs two at a time. He disappeared, checked out the rooms and then came to the top of the stairs. "Nothing."

"What the hell?"

Jones walked down and stopped near the front door. "We've been set up for some reason."

"But why?"

"I don't know, but no one lives here now."

12

IN THE SWAMPS NEAR
AP TAN HOA FOUR

When the sun set, the lights of the brothel came on. Porch, room and security lights made the building look like a beacon. Gerber was awed by the transition, surprised and amazed that something like this should exist in the swamps.

And the men kept coming. He had watched the ARVN truck leave an hour earlier, but it had been replaced by another, and when he asked Albright where the soldiers were stationed, Albright had told him at the French fort.

There were more jeeps parked around the building now that many of the Americans in the area were off duty. Again Gerber was struck by the nine-to-five nature of the war. The men on the big bases went on duty about eight and got off at four or five, just as if they held jobs in the civilian world. Apparently, once they were off duty, no one cared what they did, and many of them showed up here.

Using his binoculars, he read the unit identifications stenciled on the bumpers of the jeeps and trucks, and for a moment he wondered if he should make notes so that he could tell someone at MACV. But he dismissed the notion, thinking it would just make trouble for the lower ranking enlisted men who didn't need his help to get into trouble.

When the sun was gone, Gerber moved from under the protective branches of his bush and was surprised to find a cool breeze blowing. It was almost like moving from the heat-drenched outside into the air-conditioning of MACV Headquarters. He felt the sweat dry quickly and his skin turn itchy.

And, with the sun gone, there was only a small chance of detection. During the day there had been farmers in the fields to the north and east of them and there had been people moving on the fringes of the swamps. Some of them had been fishing, and although Gerber had expected nothing, he had seen them catching small, flat fish.

But no one had ventured near them or toward the dry ground where Fetterman hid. And it was unlikely that anyone would stroll through the swamp in the dark.

Gerber moved to the rear of his tiny island so that his feet were touching the water and he was hidden by the hump in the island's center. Protected from sight, he ate another cold meal of C-rations. It was food that he didn't taste now that his mind was on the coming events. The stuff was cardboard food processed by people who knew they would never have to eat it and who knew that the men who did would be in no position to complain. Canned food didn't have to be tasteless, but who cared if some GI in a jungle halfway around the world didn't like it?

He finished eating and cut a hole in the bottom of the can before he dropped it into the water. It filled quickly and disappeared without a sound. Then he drank from his canteen, finishing the water. It was still warm from the heat of the sun and tasted of plastic, but it relieved his thirst.

When Gerber crawled back to the front of the island, Albright touched his shoulder, then leaned close to his ear. "He's arrived."

"You sure?"

"Car by the side of the hootch is his. I saw him get out."

Gerber felt excitement bubble in his stomach now that his prey was within striking distance. He took a deep breath. "Okay. We hang loose until things slow down a little. You sure he's going to spend the night?"

"That's been his habit in the past."

Slowly Gerber rubbed a hand over his face. "Then we lay low and wait for our opportunity."

"What about Sergeant Fetterman?"

"We'll contact him later. Right now we watch the building and his car to make sure he doesn't drive away."

Gerber took the binoculars and trained them on the building. On the second-floor balcony he could see a man and a woman locked in a tight embrace. They were swaying in time to the music of AFVN that drifted over the swamp. The man moved away from the woman and then slipped her blouse from her shoulders. In the light from the bedroom, Gerber could see that she wore no bra. He realized he was seeing more naked women in the swamp than he saw in some of the seamier Saigon nightclubs.

When the man tried to slip the woman's skirt over her hips, she pushed him away and ran into the bedroom. She stood there shouting, her fists on her hips. As the man came at her, she pushed her skirt down revealing the white wisp of cloth covering her. Then she disappeared.

For more than two hours Gerber watched men arrive and no one leave. He checked the time carefully, pulling the camouflage cover from his watch to stare at the glowing hands. As it got later, the lights began to fade and the men started to leave. One or two of them dragged the naked girls onto the porch with them. There were squeals of mock outrage as the men teased them.

Soon the jeeps were pulling out frequently and the number of vehicles parked outside dwindled until there was only the truck brought by the ARVN soldiers and the car driven by their target.

It was now just after midnight. The noise from the brothel had faded along with most of the lights. Gerber slipped back across his island until he was out of sight of the building. He took the tiny portable URC-10 from his pack and turned it on. Holding it close to his ear, he adjusted the volume by listening to the carrier wave. When he was satisfied, he keyed the mike and spoke. "Band Two, this is One."

He waited, repeated the call and then heard, "Go, One."
"Target sighted. We move in one-five minutes."
"Roger."
"You have responsibility for the back. See you inside."
"Roger."

Gerber collapsed the antenna and put the radio away. He then moved to the front of the island and said, "We go in fifteen minutes. You ready?"

Albright nodded and moved to the left so that he could pass the word to the Vietnamese striker.

Gerber silently counted down the minutes, and when the time had expired he moved forward. He slipped into the water quietly, glanced to the right and saw the dark shape of Albright. He was joined by the Vietnamese striker, and all three of them began to slow-walk to the brothel.

AS SOON AS FETTERMAN received the message, he turned off his radio and stored it. He checked the time, and when fifteen minutes had elapsed he touched the striker with him and they slipped into the water. They lost sight of the building as they moved into deeper water and the grasses were over their heads, but Fetterman could still hear the music.

He stopped once, listened carefully and started again, angling toward the rear of the building. The water, which had been waist-deep, dropped away, and Fetterman slowed his pace as he neared the target. He crouched, the grass at eye level. The building loomed in front of him. He was looking at a corner of it and the rear. There was a single door there. On the ground floor there were a couple of windows and a row on the second story.

Fetterman watched the door for a moment and listened to the music. Hearing no voices, he pointed to the left, and the striker moved off. Fetterman came out of the water, stopped and then started again. He reached the corner of the building and flattened himself against it, pressing an ear to the crumbling stuccolike material that covered it. From the inside came the quiet beat of rock music and a murmur of voices.

Fetterman slid to the right, his back against the wall. He saw the striker move in the shadow, then drop to the ground. As that happened, Fetterman reached the rear door. He touched the knob and twisted it. When it turned, he let go of it and moved around it until he could look through one of the windows.

The inside was lighted by a dim red lamp. A man lay on top of a woman who had her legs wrapped around him, her feet locked together and pressed into the small of his back. She was whipping her head from side to side, moaning loudly.

Fetterman ducked back, crawled under the window and looked in from the other side. From that angle he could see the man's clothing: black pajamas, Ho Chi Minh sandals and a pouch for AK-47 magazines.

He moved on, glanced in the next window and discovered that the room was empty. Reaching out, he touched the window. It swung inward with a quiet squeak. He motioned to the striker, holding up a hand to tell the man to stay put. With that, he climbed in the window. As his feet touched the rough wood of the floor, he heard voices outside the door. To his right was a wardrobe that nearly touched the outside wall. Fetterman stepped to it and slipped into the space there, sliding down so that he was kneeling. By turning his face to the wall, he was nearly invisible in the shadows if they didn't turn on a light.

A Vietnamese man and woman entered. The man pushed the door closed and then grabbed the woman. She spun toward him and he grabbed at her blouse. He peeled her out of it and then took off her pants. As she sat on the thin cot, the man stripped and then jumped to the end of the bed, landing between her knees. He laughed as he spread her thighs and collapsed onto her.

Fetterman knew the man was one of the VC, since he had seen him arrive with their target. He wanted to kill the man, but he'd have to kill the woman, too. There was no way he could leave her alive if he was going to continue his search. He decided to wait.

The room filled with the musky odor of sex. There was a wet slapping as the two bodies thumped together. Fetterman watched the show for a moment, then, afraid that he would psychically communicate his presence to the couple, he looked away. He kept his eyes on the floor, listening to the moaning of the woman and the grunting of the man.

The tempo increased and the woman cried out. There was a single shout from the man and the pair stopped moving. They were breathing heavily.

The woman muttered something and pushed the man onto his side. She got out of bed and stood there for a moment as if to let him admire her body. Then she picked up her clothes and scampered out of the room.

The moment the door closed Fetterman unfolded himself. He drew his knife as he lunged at the bed. The man turned, startled. He began to sit up as Fetterman hit him. As the man collapsed, Fetterman clapped a hand over his nose and mouth and used the knife. There was a whisper like the ripping of silk. The man bucked once. As he died, his hot blood splashing over Fetterman's hand, there was the stench of released bowels. When the tension drained from the man, Fetterman moved away. Then, before he left the room, he pulled a sheet up so that it looked as if the man was sleeping.

At the doorway Fetterman stopped. He reached down and touched the knob. Pulling open the door, he looked out into the hallway. It was empty. For a moment he stood there, quietly waiting.

GERBER, ALBRIGHT and the Vietnamese striker worked their way toward the front of the building, keeping to the shadows and using the cover available. One by one they filtered along the edge of the swamp to the clump of bushes that was between them and one of the windows. Getting out of the water, they moved silently toward the car that the target had arrived in.

Gerber worked his way to the driver's side and looked in the open window. He wanted to open the door and rifle the glove compartment to search for documents, but was afraid of the dome light. He motioned to Albright, and when the Special Forces sergeant arrived, Gerber whispered, ''You tell your man I want him to search the car quietly once we're inside. He'll have to crawl in the window. He's to steal every scrap of paper he can find.''

Albright nodded and held up a thumb, indicating he understood. He then moved to the front of the vehicle to pass along the instructions.

Gerber and Albright then moved forward until they were lying on the ground at the base of the porch. Gerber lay with his face pressed in the dirt, inhaling the dank odor and listening to the sounds from inside the building. There was a throbbing beat from rock and roll and the discordant strains of Vietnamese music as two stereos fought for supremacy. A tickle of laughter sounded above the music.

Gerber crawled forward until he reached the corner of the porch. Slowly he got to his hands and knees and peeked over the edge of the porch. It was still vacant, the table and chairs standing empty.

He glanced over his shoulder and saw Albright waiting. Gerber motioned him to rise, and the two of them stepped up onto the porch at the edge of the pools of light. Gerber slung his weapon, then leaped up and caught hold of the balcony overhang. He lifted himself until his eyes were level with the flooring. Again there was no one around to see him.

Using the muscles of his shoulders and arms, he pulled himself higher until he could hook his foot onto the edge of the floor. His hand then shot out, and he snagged the top of the railing, lifting until his knees were on the balcony. Once he had gained it, he scrambled silently to the left and flattened himself against the rough wall, concealing himself in the shadows.

Seconds later Albright appeared, hesitated and then stepped over the railing. He dropped to one knee and pulled his rifle around so that he held it in his hands. He nodded to Gerber.

Gerber slipped along the wall until he reached the French doors that opened onto the balcony. He looked through the window. The room was empty. Crouching, he reached across the pane to the ornate, curved handle. He pulled down on it and felt it give. Without a word to Albright, he opened the door and entered.

A moment later Albright followed him. The room was dark, with only a little light filtering in through the French doors. There was the long, gray shape of the bed and a mass against one wall that might have been a wardrobe.

Gerber moved to the door and opened it slightly so that he could look out into the hallway. The rock and roll music suddenly died, and Gerber jumped back, his heart pounding. But the Vietnamese music continued. No one had heard anything. The enemy wasn't alerted.

Again he moved forward. The hallway, lighted by small lamps on the walls, was empty. Gerber opened the door wider and stepped out. He slid along the wall until he reached another door and then hesitated. The last thing he wanted to do was kill the wrong people. But he didn't know where the VC leader was. Pressing an ear against the door, he heard the unmistakable sounds of two people in the room. He moved back to the doorway.

"How do we find this guy?" asked Gerber softly.

Albright shrugged.

"Okay, then. I'll stay here and watch the hall. You get back on the balcony and peek into the windows."

Albright nodded.

As he moved to the door, Gerber, his back against the wall, stared into the hallway. At the far end, almost out of sight, he saw a shadow move and then Fetterman appeared, moving upward quietly.

Just as Fetterman reached the hallway, one of the doors opened and a man stepped out. He was a thin, short man wearing a towel wrapped around his waist.

Fetterman ducked back down the stairs and out of sight. Gerber didn't move but kept his eyes on the man.

He stood quietly, turning his head from side to side like a man watching a high-speed tennis game. He put one hand on his hip and took a deep breath. He shouted something in Vietnamese and the music died. When it did, he nodded once and turned to go back to his room. That was when Gerber saw the scar that ran from just under his left eye across his face to the right jaw. The tip of his nose was missing.

Gerber glanced at the French doors, but Albright had already disappeared through them. The Special Forces Captain opened the door wider and stepped into the hallway as Fetterman entered it at the far end. Gerber pointed to the right side of the door, and Fetterman nodded his understanding. Both of them moved forward, staying close to the wall where there was less chance of a floorboard popping.

They reached the door and flattened themselves against it. Gerber was aware that at any moment someone else could open a door and all hell would break loose. Still, he had to move carefully because they didn't want a firefight. Just a quick, quiet assassination.

When his hand touched the knob, Gerber looked at Fetterman, who nodded once. The master sergeant was ready. Slowly the captain turned the knob to its limit. Then he nodded to Fetterman, who centered himself on the door.

Gerber pushed it open, and as he did Fetterman swept into the room, his knife ready. The captain moved in behind him. There was an impression of two naked people on the bed, one on top of the other. The man came up, spinning as he did. Fetterman hit him once, and as the VC fell, the master sergeant clamped a hand over his mouth and nose. The VC leader kicked, his bare foot striking Fetterman in the hip. With one swipe, the master sergeant cut the enemy's throat. The room was immediately filled with the coppery smell of hot, fresh blood.

The woman, at first frozen in panic, came off the bed in a single, fluid motion. She dodged around Fetterman and the VC and came right at Gerber. With one hand, she tried to push him aside, and when that didn't work she opened her mouth to scream.

Gerber punched her in the stomach as hard as he could. There was a grunt of surprise and pain as the air escaped from her lungs. She dropped to the floor, her arms wrapped around her belly, her knees hiked up. Her mouth worked like that of a fish out of water as she tried to suck in some air.

Fetterman turned and pulled a stained beret from his pocket. He dropped it on the chest of the dead man and pinned it there with a Randall Combat Knife. He then looked at Gerber.

Gerber jerked the sheet from the bed and ripped a strip from it. He tore it in half, jammed part of it into the girl's mouth and used the other half to tie the first section in place.

Fetterman got the idea and tore another strip, handing it to Gerber. He used it to bind the girl's hands behind her back and then brought the end of it up to fasten her ankles so that she couldn't run out into the hallway. It would take her twenty or thirty minutes to free herself and that was plenty of time for them to get clear. With that kind of head start they could easily outdistance anyone who tried to organize a pursuit.

Together, Gerber and Fetterman moved into the hallway. They walked quickly to the room Gerber had used and then to the French doors. They stepped onto the balcony into the heat and humidity of the night. Albright saw them and moved back to them. Silently they dropped to the ground.

Fetterman broke away, heading to the rear of the building to pick up the striker hiding there. As he did, Gerber worked his way to the car. The striker appeared, holding a briefcase up like a trophy.

Now they all headed toward the swamp. They slipped into the water as Fetterman and his striker joined them. Hurrying along, they put distance between them and the house, afraid the girl would free herself and shout the alarm. But the minutes slipped by and there was no indication that anything had happened or that the body had been discovered.

For an hour they slogged their way through the swamp, moving as quickly as the water would allow them. The only noise they made was an occasional quiet splashing as they hurried. Albright stopped at a small island of dry land, but Gerber motioned him onward.

They kept at it until they reached the tree line they had used earlier. Here they fanned out in order to take a short rest. Then Gerber got them on their feet again, and they moved west, staying inside the tree line as long as they could. They reached the end of it and once more entered the swamp, continuing on through it rapidly now. Around them they could hear birds as dawn approached. Overhead, jets returning from missions roared, and there was an increased noise from helicopters.

With dawn approaching, the light from the sun smearing the horizon a fiery red, they came close to Hiep Hoa. The swamp birds were now all awake and shouting their existence to the world. The noise of dawn drowned out the other sounds.

With Hiep Hoa a dark smudge on the horizon, they stopped and waited for the sun. Gerber decided against using the radio to alert the defenders that he and his team were out there. It would only be a few minutes before the sun was up, and that would give them a chance to rest for a few moments. Gerber told them to eat the rest of their C-rations if they were hungry, or if they could wait, he'd make sure they got a good breakfast at Duc Hoa if they could get a chopper fast enough, or at Hiep Hoa if they couldn't.

When the ground around them was bright, they left their cover, moving slowly toward the perimeter. As they approached, they waited to be identified visually, then alerted the camp by radio that they were coming in.

The camp commander met them at the gate, and Gerber asked that he arrange for airlift.

"No problem. We've a morning chopper and he's due in about thirty minutes or so. I take it that your mission was a success."

"Most definitely," responded Gerber.

"Then I'll arrange your transport. We should be able to get you back to Duc Hoa in a few minutes."

"Thank you, Captain. Now if we could get a cup of coffee while we wait."

"Follow me," he said as he turned, marching toward the team house.

13

THE SPECIAL FORCES CAMP WEST OF NHA TRANG

Santini left the tiny makeshift prison where his four female prisoners waited and walked out into the middle of the compound. He had been surprised to learn that the camp had three other female prisoners; then he wondered about that. Obviously the VC were equal opportunity employers. The sun was up high enough so that the buildings were a dark gray and the ground was a gray pool. He could see dark objects, a pile of sandbags, the bottom half of a fifty-five-gallon drum and a tire for a jeep scattered around. Beyond all that was the bunker line where the entire camp had been on alert since midnight. But nothing had happened.

As he neared the gate in the redoubt, Captain Bundt loomed out of the grayness. "How are the prisoners?" he inquired.

"I've got them locked in. Nothing, huh?"

Bundt shook his head. "It's always been reliable before. The civilians don't arrive and we get mortared sometime in the next twenty-four hours. Couple that with what your girl is telling us and I was sure something was going to happen tonight."

"What time do the civilians arrive?"

Bundt held the underside of his wrist up in front of his face so that he could look at his watch. "I'd say they should begin arriving in about thirty minutes."

Santini turned and looked back toward the tiny structure where the female prisoners were grouped. He then looked toward the village, situated a half a klick from the camp. In the half-light of dawn, the mist squeezed from air that was heavy with moisture, there was nothing to see. It was as if the mist had swallowed the village.

"If they don't get here?"

"Then the assumption would be that something big is going to happen. I might take my intel NCO downtown and see if we can learn anything."

"And that'd work?"

Bundt shrugged. "Who knows? There are many people who are loyal to us but who don't want to be around when the enemy starts dropping mortars."

"They could warn you."

"But they do. The fact that they don't show up warns us. It means someone has been around telling them there will be some kind of operation directed toward us. What more do we need to know?"

"Time and location."

Again Bundt shrugged. "So before today it meant we could expect the attack within twenty-four hours, usually sooner. Today is different."

"Okay, sir," said Santini. "I was thinking of heading back to Nha Trang today."

"I hate to lose you. We can always use the extra weapon and the extra man, but I understand. You going to take your prisoner with you?"

"I thought I'd leave her here. I don't like what those Vietnamese interrogators at Nha Trang were doing. She'll be safe here."

"What do you plan to say once you get back to Nha Trang?"

Santini rubbed his face and felt the stubble. His eyes felt like someone had thrown a handful of sand into them. He blinked rapidly. "I'm going to tell them that my prisoner suggested something is going to happen soon. I'm going to tell them what has happened here, that the civilians didn't show up, and that the men in the field are getting worried.''

Bundt switched his weapon from his right hand to his left. He surveyed his camp slowly. ''Yeah, I think we're getting real uncomfortable. Charlie is planning something. You can feel it in the air.''

''The thing that worries me, sir, is that everyone seems to have that feeling.''

JEWELL MET GERBER'S TEAM at the helipad at Duc Hoa. He waited until the helicopter took off in a thunder of engine noise and popping rotor blades. As the silence of early morning descended, Jewell asked, ''How'd it go?''

''Fine. We got the man.'' Gerber grinned. ''Sergeant Fetterman added a nice touch. Left a green beret pinned to the chest of the target so that everyone knows why it happened and who did it.''

Jewell looked at Fetterman. ''Well-done, Sergeant.''

''Yeah. I didn't want the wrong people getting the credit for it.''

''Can't hurt.'' Jewell pointed toward the team house. ''You gentlemen eat breakfast yet?''

''No,'' said Gerber. ''I promised the team a good breakfast when we got in here. I hope you're not going to make a liar out of me.''

Albright stepped forward. ''Sir, we've got a briefcase that was in the car. It's loaded with papers. I thought maybe Sergeant Prewitt should take a quick look at it. If there's anything of interest in it, Captain Gerber and Sergeant Fetterman can take it to Saigon with them.''

Jewell nodded. ''By the way, I'll have to arrange for airlift. Didn't know when you'd be coming in.''

''That's fine,'' said Gerber. ''I'd like to grab a shower, if that's possible. Clean up a little.''

''Water'll be cold this early,'' said Jewell, ''but you're certainly welcome to it.''

''Thanks. Point me in the right direction.''

"Come with me," said Albright. "We'll swing by my quarters for soap and towels."

"And give me the briefcase," said Jewell. "I'll see that Sergeant Prewitt gets it."

Gerber and Fetterman followed Albright. He got them everything they needed and then left them in the shower. Ten minutes later he was back with clean clothes drawn from the base supply.

After another fifteen minutes, they were all gathered in the team house. Albright and the two Vietnamese strikers took over the duties of setting the table and putting the food on it. Once that was completed, they all sat down to cold cereal, scrambled eggs, toast and jelly, and coffee and orange juice. The food wasn't as good as it was at the MACV Headquarters mess hall, but then, Duc Hoa didn't have a general officer to keep happy.

They were halfway through the meal when Jewell, accompanied by Sergeant Prewitt, joined them. Prewitt looked upset. His face was pale.

Jewell pulled a chair away from another table and sat down so that the corner of the table was pointed at his stomach. He leaned forward. "That stuff you found is dynamite."

"What is it?"

"It's an order of battle drawn up by our recently late friend. It details a plan to attack us here, at Duc Hoa, plus the camps at the sugar mill and Hiep Hoa, not to mention assaults directed at the leg outfit at the old French fort."

"Jesus H. Christ on a pogo stick," said Gerber.

"I mean, it's a detailed plan. Gives the names of the units to be involved and who's supposed to do what. Prewitt didn't go through much of it. He thinks you'd better get this to Saigon so they can evaluate it."

Gerber nodded his agreement. "When does all of this start?"

"Not long. During Tet. The beginning of Tet."

"Who all is involved?"

"Our guy was a local, so he's only got the plans for the local area, but the whole place is involved. I think we can assume it's a widespread plan."

Gerber wiped his lips with his napkin and dropped it onto the table. "I think we'd better get this stuff to Saigon as quickly as we can."

"I thought you'd say that," said Jewell. "I took the liberty of arranging a chopper. Should be here about the time we get to the runway."

Gerber looked at Fetterman. "If you're through, Master Sergeant."

"Yes, sir. Ready." He stood.

Jewell picked up the briefcase. "Everything's in here."

As they left the team house, they heard the helicopter coming in. Over the tin roofs of the hootches they could see it. As they neared the runway, it flared, stirring up a huge cloud of red dust. Gerber and Fetterman ducked their heads and ran for the chopper. Once they were in, Gerber clutching the briefcase in one hand and his weapon in the other, the aircraft lifted off. It crossed the perimeter wires, climbing out. Before it reached the river, it broke around to the east, heading for Saigon.

It seemed to be only minutes before they were diving under the runway approaches at Tan Son Nhut. They landed at Hotel Three, and almost as the skids touched the ground, both Gerber and Fetterman were off and running. They ran past the terminal, through the gate and around the edge of the field, skirting the World's Largest PX. In minutes they had secured a jeep and were racing through the morning traffic, dodging military convoys, MPs in jeeps, the *cao bois* on their Hondas and all the pedestrian traffic.

At MACV Headquarters they hesitated for a moment, wondering if they should pass the briefcase to Jerry Maxwell, the local CIA spook, or if they should keep it in the family. Finally they ran upstairs and found the office of Major General Davidson. He had ordered them into the field more than once on sensitive missions.

In his outer office, a big room with powder-blue carpeting on the floor, dark wood paneling on the walls and three large wooden desks, they were stopped by a major who demanded to know the nature of their business.

Gerber held up the briefcase but didn't speak right away. He was wondering where they all came from. Here was a major who looked as if a stiff breeze would blow him away. His skin was pale, as if he never got out into the sun. His black hair was chopped short as military regulations said it should be. He had a long, pointed nose and a pointed chin. There were a couple of razor scratches on his face, suggesting that he had tried to shave too close with a dull blade.

Finally Gerber said, "Listen. We've come across some information that we thought the general would want."

"Do you have an appointment?" asked the major as he flipped through the appointment calendar on his desk.

"Major," said Gerber with great patience, "I think you had better alert the general that Captain Gerber and Sergeant Fetterman are here to see him. If you don't I'll take this down to Maxwell and your ass will be out of here."

"I don't respond well to threats," said the major evenly.

"Fine. Then consider it a request, but please do it."

For a moment the major stood there staring at Gerber, but when the captain didn't back down, the major spun and entered the inner office. He closed the door but returned a few seconds later.

"You may go in," he said.

Gerber and Fetterman entered the office to find Davidson sitting behind his desk. He was working on a stack of papers. He signed one and then looked up. "What do you have?"

"I would like someone to look at these papers," said Gerber. "The indications are that the enemy is building up in Hau Nghia Province and that they plan to launch an attack."

Davidson rocked back in his chair and laced his hands behind his head. He sighed deeply and asked, "When will this happen?"

"Beginning of Tet."

"Shit. Just one more thing to go wrong."

14

THE WIRE SERVICE
BUREAU, DOWNTOWN
SAIGON

Robin Morrow sat quietly at her desk looking at the notes she had gathered during the day. Interviews with high-ranking officers who suggested that nothing was going to happen soon, but using very guarded language that said they knew something more. Interviews with the top civilians in Saigon, politicians and political appointees who were parroting Washington's belief that the war was winding down. These men, and a few women, honestly believed what they had been saying, but Morrow hadn't. And finally there were interviews with low-ranking officers and NCOs who were walking around like condemned men. There was definitely something in the air.

She flipped through the pages again. Using a light blue pencil, she crossed out the nonsense given to her by the politicians and some of that spouted by the officers at MACV who were protecting the autumn of their careers. In the end she was left with the distinct impression that something was going to happen, and it was only hours away, Tet truce or no Tet truce.

Finally she turned and looked toward the rear of the room where Crown sat impatiently, reading from the notes he had taken. He glanced up and saw that Morrow's eyes were on him. He lifted his eyebrows in question.

She waved at him. "Get over here."

Slowly he got to his feet and walked across the floor, avoiding the wastebasket that someone had set in the aisle between the desks. He pulled the chair from the vacant desk next to hers and straddled it, his arms resting on the back.

"What?" he asked.

"What?" she repeated. "You didn't notice anything about all that we learned today."

"Only that what Mr. Hodges said is probably correct. This thing is about to end."

Morrow rolled her eyes at the ceiling and then stared straight at him. "Didn't you listen to what was said today?"

"Of course. I heard the ambassador saying that the enemy hasn't launched any kind of an attack in weeks. . . ."

"Except at Khe Sanh."

"Yeah. The last gasp of the dying enemy. That's what the ambassador said."

"Yeah," said Morrow. "And there've been mortar attacks on Special Forces camps and there was a helicopter shot down near Tay Ninh."

"Sporadic resistance that doesn't mean anything. The generals over at MACV have said that they see the light at the end of the tunnel."

"I don't know what reporting is coming to," said Morrow quietly. "Those generals are political appointees. General officers have their promotions approved by Congress. The Administration in Washington is saying that the war is winding down and the generals don't want to rock the boat. They repeat what the Administration says."

Crown snorted. "Then who do you believe? Some rummy sergeant who is so dumb that after twenty years in the Army he's still only a sergeant?"

Morrow thought of Fetterman, one of the brightest men she knew, a man who enjoyed the limited authority his rank gave him and who wanted to remain right where he was because he was doing the job he wanted to. There was no incentive for

Fetterman to get a promotion, because to do so would remove
him from the field.

To Crown, she said, "Given a choice between the sergeant
who's been in the field and the general who's been in his air-
conditioned office, I'll take the sergeant. I tell you something
is going to happen soon and it's going to be big."

"That's right Robin," said a voice behind her. "You stick
with that when all the facts point the other way." Hodges
moved forward so that she could see him.

She grabbed her notebook and held it high. "Not everyone
is convinced that the war is nearly over. I've . . . we've talked
to a number of men who think that Charlie is about to fall on
us like a ton of bricks."

"And who are these men with the crystal balls?" sneered
Hodges.

"I've got interviews with Sergeant Nubumb, Lopez and a
Captain Padgett. All of them think that something is about to
happen."

"And the generals?" said Hodges. "They don't agree, do
they? And who should we believe? Some sergeant or the
general who has all the information at his fingertips?"

"I'll take the sergeant any day of the week and twice on
Sunday," said Morrow, "if he's been in the field looking for
the enemy." She thought about all the things that had been
played down recently. The big fight in the Hobo Woods, the
assault on the Special Forces camp at Plei Soi and now the attack on Khe Sanh. It was obviously the beginning of something, but no one wanted to see it.

LE TRAN, DRESSED in an *ao dai* and looking like a petite
Vietnamese girl out for a stroll by herself after dark, walked
slowly toward the cemetery. Around her the city was awake
and beginning to celebrate. The Saigon government, the
puppet of the Americans, had declared that the normal curfew would not be in effect during the Tet holidays. There were
hundreds, thousands of people on the streets.

Le Tran turned away from the lurid neon and the noise of
the bars and entered a quiet, peaceful street. She could hear

the sounds of the city: a car horn in the hot, humid air, the roar of a motorcycle as a *cao bois* clamored for attention. Le Tran smiled to herself. The hooligans of Saigon would soon be in their places.

At the cemetery gate she stopped and looked at the rows of grave markers. Here was a neat, well-kept park for the dead, with money spent on people who had no appreciation of it, money that could have gone to the sick and the homeless and the poor, if the people understood the diseases of society. After tonight that would all change.

The lock on the gate had been broken, and Le Tran knew that some of the men were now in the graveyard, waiting for her. She opened the gate, being careful not to make any noise, and then closed it quietly. For a moment she stood there, staring into the palm-lined street, waiting for a shout or the running feet of someone who had spotted her entering where she didn't belong, but no one came and no one shouted.

She then crossed the cemetery and made her way over a slight rise that hid her from the street. In the distance, near a grove of carefully groomed palms, she saw a couple of figures hunched over. She knew that they were digging up a gravesite that was only a couple of weeks old. She had been at the funeral and knew that no corpse had been contained in the polished wooden coffin.

She moved toward them rapidly, and when they heard her approaching, they dived for cover. She stopped and then started forward more slowly, giving the men time to recognize her. When there was a quiet whistle, she hurried toward them.

"Almost there," one of them whispered.

She nodded and stood back as a shovel struck the hard wood of the coffin. One of the men dropped into the hole and used his hands to claw at the loose dirt. Another of the men tossed him the end of a rope, which he tied around the handles of the coffin. He leaped clear as three other men began to muscle the box out of the ground.

As it came clear with a scraping of wood and rustle of loose dirt cascading into the hole, there was a sudden, low rumble from the street. Le Tran spun, but saw nothing at first. Then she climbed to the top of the rise and saw the blackened shadows of the front gate. Beyond it was a military jeep, an M-60 machine gun mounted in the back.

She turned and hissed at the men. "Stay down. Stay quiet. American MPs."

She stood still, waiting, but the jeep didn't drive off. Instead a small light appeared, the beam focused on the ruined lock.

Someone appeared beside her and handed her a pistol. She glanced down at it and wanted to check it, but knew that the action couldn't be concealed.

"It is ready," whispered the man lying on the ground beside her. "Round chambered and safety off."

Le Tran started toward the gate, moving slowly, the weapon now concealed at her side. Behind the light were two MPs, examining the lock. One of them pushed on the iron, and the gate swung open. They spotted Le Tran, and one of the flashlight beams stabbed out toward her.

"What are you doing here?" demanded the bigger man.

She pretended she didn't hear and kept walking toward them. There was a burst of static from the radio in their jeep, and one of the men turned toward it.

"I come to see father," said Le Tran suddenly. The MP who had started to the jeep stopped.

"You're not supposed to be here after dark," said the MP. "The gate is locked at dusk."

"Gate no locked," she said. "I push. It open."

"Yes, well." The MP moved away from the gate toward her. The shiny black helmet he wore reflected the dim lights from the street. He had a rifle slung over his shoulder and a pistol on his hip. He looked bulky, as if he was barrel-chested, but it was the flak jacket he wore. It wasn't bulletproof, but it would slow down almost everything unless fired from extremely close range and it would stop shrapnel.

"Come on," he said politely. "We'll give you a ride home. You shouldn't be on the streets tonight, alone."

As she neared them, wishing they would stay together, the other MP shouted. "She's got a gun!"

She snapped her hand up and opened fire. The muzzle-flash reached out and touched the chest of the MP. He grunted with surprise and sat down, clawing at the flap on his holster as she fired again, this time at his face. He flipped back and didn't move.

An automatic weapon erupted. Le Tran heard the rounds snap by her. There was a wet slap of impact. The second MP collapsed. He groaned, rolled to his side and lay still.

Le Tran jumped forward and took the pistol from the dead American. She stripped the rifle from his shoulder and pulled the combat knife from the scabbard. She moved to the second man and realized that he wasn't dead. There was a black puddle of blood near him. The breath rasped in his throat as he fought to breathe.

She stood over him. It was clear that he was unconscious, moaning in pain. She aimed the pistol, holding it in both hands. As she pulled the trigger, the muzzle-flash illuminated his features. A young man with light hair and a light mustache. He spasmed once as the bullet slammed into his head and punched out the back of his skull.

One of the men joined her. She whispered to him. "You grab his weapons. It was nice of the Americans to donate to our cause."

"We have to get out of here," warned the man.

"Why?" She gestured at the darkened sky. They could see lines of red tracers dancing upward in celebration. There were now bursts of firecrackers sounding like small-arms fire. The detonation of fireworks punctuated the sounds of the city. "No one will notice."

As she spoke, the rest of the men approached, carrying the coffin they had dug up. They hurried to the gate and stopped.

"We'll take the Americans' machine gun and ammo, too," she said. "One of you go get it."

As the men scrambled to obey her orders, she looked at the bodies once more. Two Americans dead already and the enemy didn't know what was happening. A good omen.

And then, at the corner, she noticed the flashing of a red light above the silhouette of a jeep. There were two small slits on the headlights providing very little illumination. Le Tran knew that someone was coming to check on the jeep and the firing. They'd have to leave the machine gun.

"Let's go," she whispered. They vanished into the shadows with the weapons from the grave and those taken from the bodies of the Americans as the second jeep skidded to a halt behind the first.

THE FIRST MORTAR ROUND fell short, exploding in the wire outside the camp. Bromhead heard the *crump* in the distance and ran to the doorway. He stopped there, listening, waiting for the second one. It was closer than the first but still outside the camp, in the wire. Bromhead didn't see the flash of the explosion.

He leaped to his feet and ran between two buildings. Leaving the redoubt, he scrambled up the ladder of the fire control tower. There was no one there. Snatching the handset of the field phone from the cradle, he spun the crank once and heard the communications sergeant answer immediately.

"Wait one," ordered Bromhead. He set the phone down and crouched to open the case containing the binoculars. As he straightened up, the mortars began to fall again, this time on the compound. He saw the flashes as they detonated, looking like fountains of sparks. He began to scan the horizon around his camp, the thick jungle north and west and the hills to the east. He kept searching as more enemy shells landed. Out of the corner of his eye he caught the flickering of flames as some of the hootches started to burn. There was a rattling around him as the shrapnel from the mortars struck the tower.

In the north he caught a single flash when a mortar fired. He grabbed the field phone, his eyes locked on the target. "Pit One, Pit Two, I have a fire mission."

When they answered, he gave them the range and direction of the enemy weapon. He told them what charge to use and waited until they fired in response to the enemy. The rounds dropped short of the enemy tube and Bromhead made corrections.

But as he did, more enemy rounds fell on the camp. Explosions began to blossom all over as the enemy gunners found the range. Bromhead didn't pay attention to the damage being done to his camp. He kept watching for the enemy, and each time he spotted them he brought more of his weapons to bear.

SANTINI WAS IN THE NCO club at Nha Trang when the first of the mortar rounds fell. Because of the noise of the jukebox no one in the club heard the first explosions. The rounds dropped across the runway in the Air Force area.

Then came a searing note that cut through the pounding jukebox and the shouting of the men. The single loud note sounded like the horn of an angry driver in rush-hour traffic. Quiet fell like a curtain and someone pulled the plug on the jukebox.

"Everyone to the bunkers," shouted one of the sergeants unnecessarily.

The men crowded forward toward the only door as the explosions started again. Men dived right and left under the tables and chairs. Two men rolled close to the bar, and the bartender disappeared behind it. It looked as if the club had been carpeted with men.

Santini listened from his position in a corner, his head stuck under a chair. The car horn faded, but the mortars kept falling. They were walking away from him, moving toward the center of the base.

But then came another sound—a loud, flat bang that hurt his ears and shook dirt from the parachute canopies hung in the rafters. The smell of cordite filled the air, and Santini knew that the enemy was using rockets, too.

Now he wished he could get out. Mortars didn't scare him— they were small, ineffective weapons that could be neutralized easily—but rockets were different. Once launched they couldn't be guided. They landed at random and had more punch than a mortar. They could blow up the entire club and kill everyone in it.

Santini crawled toward the door, climbing over a sergeant who had pressed his face to the floor and wrapped his arms around his head. Santini felt the sweat on his face and on his sides. He was breathing heavily as he worked his way forward.

As he neared the door, he felt a breeze. Outside, the mortars were still falling. He could hear them near the center of the base. A siren from a fire truck was wailing and men were shouting. From the perimeter came the hammering of the heavier weapons—the fifties were chugging.

There was a single, tremendous crash as the artillery on Nha Trang fired in response. As the shells roared outward, the lights in the club snapped off.

"What the hell?" shouted someone.

"Reducing the target," rasped another.

Santini reached the door and peered out. Nha Trang was almost completely dark. None of the normal lights were on and only the flickering of fires lit the area. To the right, one building was burning out of control, the flames shooting into the night sky. And around them the mortars continued to fall.

Santini decided he had to get out. He had to make contact with the SF camps around Nha Trang to see if they were experiencing enemy action. He needed to coordinate the information so that Major Madden would know what to do if calls for help came.

He got to his knees, watching the ground in front of him. One man ran by bent over as if opposing a stiff wind, his hand pressing down his helmet.

As Santini started to make his move, several mortars fell. He dropped to his stomach as the shrapnel riddled the side of the club. There was a crash above and behind him and one man screamed in pain.

"I'm hit," shouted another. "I'm hit."

"Let's get out of here."

Suddenly everyone was on his feet, pushing, shoving, fighting to get out of the door. Santini was pushed from behind, and he stumbled forward, his feet missing the steps. He tried to leap but failed and fell to the ground. Around him the men stampeded, shouting and shoving, trying to get to the bunkers.

The mortars fell as if aimed. There were more screams and cries of anguish as men dropped and others dived.

"Medic! Medic!" shouted one man over and over, although there were no medics around.

Santini crawled toward another man who lay on his side, his hands on his knee. He was whimpering and mumbling, his eyes closed tightly.

The sergeant pushed the man's hands out of the way and looked at the bloodstained pants. He held the knee steady and studied it. Shrapnel was stuck there. Santini could see it glinting in the flickering firelight. He reached down and touched the shrapnel. The man flinched and grabbed at Santini, who pushed his hands aside.

"Keep still," he ordered. He then gripped the metal and added, "You're going to be okay."

Santini yanked the shrapnel free. The man shrieked in pain and surprise. The sergeant pressed his hand against the man's knee as the blood began to flow freely. "You'll be okay," he said. "Just push here." He took the man's hands and put them against the wound.

Through clenched teeth, the man said, "Thanks."

"Yeah." Santini got up and started for the protection of the buildings. He slid to a halt, his back against the rough wood of a hootch. There were now flares overhead—bright points of light swinging under parachutes. These were tossed out of aircraft and stayed up longer than those fired from artillery. The ground around him was now wrapped in an eerie orange-yellow light.

Wounded littered the ground near the club. For a moment Santini thought he should stay, but there was plenty of help. Two men carrying medical bags had arrived and were treating the wounded.

There was nothing there for Santini to do. Instead, he ran between the buildings. One, on the left, was nothing more than a smoking ruin. He stopped long enough to make sure no one was in it who could be helped, then continued on, running to the side of a long one-story building that was a supply depot. He stopped there and listened. Artillery going out.

First a crash that drowned out all other noise and then the sound of a freight train overhead. And, from the perimeter, small-arms fire. Santini wondered if there was anyone to shoot at, or if they were just firing at shadows.

He ran across Nha Trang until he reached the Fifth Special Forces Headquarters. Once, he stopped to listen and realized that the mortars had ceased for the moment. Then they started again, far across the base, apparently landing in the Navy area on the bay.

Santini ran into the building and found Madden. The front of his uniform was dirty as if he had spent some time on the ground. Santini grinned at him.

Madden ignored that. "Glad you could make it."

"Me, too," said Santini. "I wasn't sure I would."

"Grab your gear and we'll decide what we're going to do."

"Yes, sir."

15

THE WIRE SERVICE BUREAU, DOWNTOWN SAIGON

Robin Morrow was sick of it all, sick of the men who thought they knew more about military operations than the military, or more about national policy than the Administration. She was sick of hearing about the end of the war and how with the Tet truce coming there wouldn't be anything to do. And most of all she was sick of the poker game going on in the corner of the room.

She was still trying to concentrate on her notes and ignore the laughter being generated by the game when one of the newest staff members ran in. He waved the tear sheets from the teletype around his head like a banner as he announced, "All hell is breaking loose."

The poker players didn't stop, but Morrow got to her feet. She yelled at the man, "What are you talking about?"

He slid to a halt and looked at the senior men still engrossed in their poker. He turned to Morrow. "Reports of mortar attacks all over the place. Reports of large numbers of VC hitting targets everywhere. Large forces moving on Hue, Da Lat and Quang Tri. The base at Nha Trang is under attack and there are ground forces moving in on Song Be."

Hodges dropped his cards and stood. "What are you saying?"

"The enemy is attacking all over the place, sir. Hundreds of them. Thousands."

"Good Christ." He shot a glance at Morrow. "You sure?"

"The reports are coming in from all over."

Hodges ran a hand through his hair. "Okay. Okay," he said, thinking fast. "We've got to get some people on this now. Got to get someone over to MACV."

"That's mine," said Morrow. "I was there all day talking to people and it's only fair."

"I want someone with a better military background," said Hodges.

"You mean one of the geniuses here who couldn't see the truth. Someone who didn't believe this was going to happen," she snapped.

"I want to confirm this before we go off half-cocked."

There was a sudden burst of machine gun fire from the street below. The men rushed to the window and looked down. A single ARVN soldier was weaving drunkenly. He carried an M-16, and as the reporters watched, he fired another burst.

"There!" yelled Hodges. "There's your problem. It's got to be like that all over South Vietnam tonight. Drunks celebrating Tet. A couple of wire service guys got nervous and put things on the machine."

Morrow took the tear sheet from the hand of the young man. She read it quickly and shook her head. "I'm afraid not. Too much detail here. The attack has begun."

Again Hodges ran a hand through his hair. He looked at the smear of grease on his palm and wiped it on his shirt. "Okay, Morrow, you think this is a big story, you hotfoot it over to MACV and see what they're doing."

She reached down and plucked her camera bag from under her desk. "I'll be glad to."

"Check in with me every thirty minutes, even if there's nothing to report." He stopped talking as another machine gun fired. This one was farther away and was quickly joined by others. It began to sound as if the war had broken out again.

"I remember Tet last year," said Hodges. "Shooting all over the fucking place. MPs racing around the city with their sirens blaring trying to find out what was happening. It was just the Vietnamese celebrating their new year."

"You get reports of mortar attacks on American bases? You get reports that the provincial capitals were being overrun? You get any of that?"

Hodges shook his head. "No. Just shooting all over the place."

Morrow shouldered her camera bag and started toward the door. "Then this is something new. You'll see."

Hodges had lost his confident look. He turned toward the window and stared into the darkness of the Vietnamese night. Behind him someone turned out the overhead lights so that only the desk lamps remained on. Far in the distance they could see lines of ruby tracers leaping into the air. Hundreds of weapons were firing. Flares burst over the city, but that wasn't anything uncommon.

Uncertainly he turned to stare at Morrow. "It's just like last year."

"Sure it is. Just like last year." She spun and hit the door with the heel of her hand. She ran down the steps and stopped at the door that led outside. For an instant she wasn't sure she wanted to venture out onto the streets but then decided that she was a reporter. She had to go out.

She opened the door and was struck by the heat and humidity. Even late at night it was muggy, the moisture in the air coating her before she could move to the curb.

Around her the city seemed to be a living entity. Thousands of people were in the streets, shouting and laughing, singing and drinking. The celebrations had spilled from the parties and the bars, filling the streets. With the curfew canceled, there was no reason to go inside.

She fought her way through the crowds. Over the merriment she could hear shooting. There were explosions that could have been enemy rockets doing damage, or friendly rockets fired in the celebration. Tracers, all of them ruby-colored, filled the night skies.

She hurried along one street, staying close to the walls of the buildings so that she could get through the crowds. People were dancing on the sidewalks. They were handing bottles of beer and fifths of wine to one another. They had abandoned all concerns of the war and most of the inhibitions of society for the night.

As she came to an alley, a machine gun opened fire near her. She felt her heart leap into her throat and her stomach flip over. When she danced back out of the way, she caught a glimpse of the muzzle-flashes and realized it was a string of firecrackers. Breathing easier, but with her hands still shaking, she hurried on.

There was a roar overhead and then a loud bang. Smoke filled the street, and Morrow could smell cordite. The revelers around her stared upward, but they didn't settle down. She wasn't sure if it had been an enemy rocket directed into the city, or a fireworks display that had malfunctioned. She pushed her way through the crowd, crossed the street and turned. The upper floor of a building was now engulfed in flames, but no one on the street cared.

Now she hesitated. She didn't want to walk in all the way to MACV and she didn't want to return to the office. She knew Hodges would be sitting in his office looking smug if she returned. It would be an opportunity for him to tell her that he had told her so. That was the last thing she wanted.

Instead, she pressed into the crowd, looking at the faces. Most of them were happy, but a few were grim, determined. She studied those people and noticed that most of them wore a red armband. She didn't know what that meant.

FETTERMAN STOOD OUTSIDE Gerber's door and pounded on it. When the captain finally opened it, Fetterman said, "We've got orders to head for MACV."

"What's the problem?"

Fetterman raised an eyebrow. "Can't you hear?"

Gerber cocked his head to one side. "I hear M-60s and M-16s, but no enemy weapons. Those are the celebrants."

"Yes, sir. Well, those attacks that we've been worried about have been launched all over South Vietnam and we're wanted at MACV."

"Okay." Gerber spun, leaving his door open. He moved into his room and grabbed his fatigue jacket off the back of a chair. As he donned it, he continued to the wardrobe set against one wall. He finished buttoning his shirt and then took his weapon out. First he checked that there was no round chambered and that the safety was on.

"Anytime, Captain."

Gerber smiled and picked up his steel pot. He looked at the pistol belt with its canteens, first-aid kit and pistol. At first he was going to leave it, but the increasing volume of firing on the streets worried him. He picked up the belt and then moved toward Fetterman.

"Let's go."

"Yes, sir."

Together they headed to the hotel lobby. It was nearly deserted. The desk clerk had left his post and was standing near the windows, watching the show outside. He didn't bother to turn as Gerber and Fetterman passed through the lobby.

They pushed open the doors, the doorman having been swept away in a crowd of merrymakers. On the street they hesitated, and Fetterman said, "I can probably get to the jeep."

"That would be nice."

"Take us forever to penetrate this crowd."

"Sergeant, I don't think we should walk to MACV. Besides, there is an old Army saying that you never walk when you can ride."

"And the pilots say that you never ride when you can fly."

"But since we don't have a chopper handy, the best we can do is ride."

"Yes, sir."

Fetterman began to push into the crowd, forcing the people to the side. As he moved deeper into them, there was a burst of firing. It wasn't a string of firecrackers or the trigger-happy fingers of ARVN soldiers. This was an AK-47. The sound ripped through the night around them.

The humid air was filled with cries of pain. People panicked, shoving one another to the side. Some fell, the others swarming over them. A second burst set them into hysterics.

Fetterman pressed himself against the wall of the building and then crouched. He turned slowly, scanning the rooftops, figuring that the sniper would be up there. He saw no movement. But the windows facing him were loaded with people hanging out and watching the drama on the street. The sniper had a perfect cover there.

Gerber loomed out of the half-light on the street. "You see anything?"

"No, sir. Thought he might be on the roof, but who can tell now?"

Gerber touched his lips with the back of his hand while his eyes continued to search. "I think we can put off that trip to MACV for a few minutes."

"Yes, sir." Fetterman moved deeper into the shadows, his eyes searching the rooftops. He caught a flicker of movement near the wall on top of the building opposite him. "Got him."

"Where?"

"Straight across the street. On top of the building, near that square. Just to the right of the corner."

"There's nothing there now," said Gerber.

"No, sir. But he was."

"How do you want to handle this?"

"Well, sir, I thought you could cover me while I cross the street. Then, if you move into the alley and use the fire escape to get to higher ground, I'll go up to the roof."

"Okay. Go when you're ready."

Fetterman didn't move immediately. He took in the scene around him. People were huddled in the shadows and behind the cars. Others lay facedown in the gutters, afraid to move. The street had taken on the deserted look of a ghost town. Lights had gone out and the music had stopped. Broken glass littered the sidewalk and the street. The only noise came from a slow leak in a car's tire.

Beyond that, on the other streets, the celebration continued. There was rock music, country and western and Vietnamese. Under all that was the murmur of voices as people partied. But in front of him there was silence.

Fetterman eased off the safety, using his thumb. He glanced at the rooftop and then sprinted across the street. As he reached the building, he spun, flattening his back against it. His head was tilted up so that he could study the overhang, but there was still no movement.

Gerber began to move then, keeping to the shadows. He reached the corner of the building and disappeared into the darkness. A moment later there was movement on the fire escape as the captain edged toward the high ground.

With that, Fetterman slipped toward the door. The master sergeant knew the man could have left the rooftop by now. He could be working his way down the stairs, so Fetterman had to be careful. He peeked in the window and saw that the first floor was empty: tables and chairs and the debris of a party. Everyone had left, but Fetterman didn't know if it was because of the shooting, or if they had taken their celebration elsewhere.

Cautiously he entered the building, the muzzle of his weapon pointing at the ceiling. He kept his back pressed against the wall as he moved to the rear of the structure. There was a beaded curtain with a light shining behind it. No one seemed to be in the hallway.

Fetterman pushed through the curtain and stopped. The hall was lined with doors, all of them closed. The proper procedure was to kick in each door, but that would take too long and the odds were that the sniper was either still on the roof or fleeing across the buildings. Fetterman didn't like leaving all those hiding places unchecked, but he couldn't do anything about it.

The master sergeant moved on, keeping his left shoulder against the wall and listening for sounds behind him. He stepped over a broken chair and a folded bamboo mat. Ignoring the broken glass that covered the floor, he kept his eyes on the stairway at the far end.

There was a sudden noise behind him. Fetterman dropped to his left knee and spun. He threw his rifle to his shoulder and sighted.

A girl dressed in an *ao dai* peeked into the hall. She took one step and saw Fetterman. Her eyes widened in fright, and she leaped back, slamming the door and bolting it.

Fetterman released his breath. Slowly, feeling like an old man, he got to his feet, looking up so that he could see to the top floor. Nothing.

Staying to the side, away from the railing, he started up slowly. Again he knew he should be checking each floor, but he didn't have the time. He kept moving higher, listening for an ambush. His shoulders were suddenly stiff from the tension. As he reached the last landing, he told himself to relax. He rolled his shoulders, but knew he couldn't relax until he knew the sniper was no longer on the roof.

Finally he reached the door. Keeping his right hand on the pistol grip of his M-16, he touched the locking bar. As he started to push it, he realized he would be silhouetted by the light behind him. He stepped back and used the barrel of his weapon to smash the light bulb. There was a quiet pop and a flash of white light. The stairwell was now in shadow.

Fetterman hesitated, his eyes closed. He listened to the sounds around him, but there was none from either the roof or the stairs. Opening his eyes, he blinked rapidly and then turned so that he could open the door, crouching low as he pushed. As the door moved, Fetterman kept the pressure slow and steady. He waited for a bullet to slam into the door, but nothing happened.

When he could squeeze through, he moved forward again, stepping into the humidity of the tropical night. For some reason, as he left the building, he had expected a cool breeze, but he was disappointed. He slipped to the left and let the door close quietly. Keeping low and scanning the rooftop, he stayed where he was.

A three-foot-high wall ran around the edge of the building and gave the sniper perfect cover. Although the roof was covered with broken furniture, ripped boxes, tin cans and newspapers, there was nothing large enough to conceal the sniper.

Fetterman eased away from the rooftop entrance and saw something move in the shadows at the far end. He froze, his head turned slightly so that he could see out of the corner of his eye. The lump in the shadows shifted again and seemed to come apart so that there was the distinct outline of a human holding an AK-47.

Fetterman raised his own weapon, looking over the top of the sights. He waited. The master sergeant wasn't a police officer about to arrest a criminal; he was a soldier who had found an enemy soldier. There were several responses, but he was in a crowded city with thousands of innocent people around. The sniper had already demonstrated that he had no regard for the innocent.

Fetterman squeezed the trigger. He felt the weapon buck against his shoulder and saw the muzzle-flash stab into the dark. There was a wet slap, and the figure grunted in surprise. The enemy sniper started to push himself up and then fell flat.

Fetterman stood, his rifle pointed at the enemy. He watched him for a moment and then let his eyes roam the roof looking for a second or third enemy, but the roof was deserted.

The sniper didn't move. Fetterman crouched near him and grabbed the AK. There was no resistance from the dead fingers. Quickly Fetterman searched the body. He found two spare banana magazines, two Chicom grenades and a map of the roof, then he turned the body over.

The sniper was wearing a white shirt with the top button fastened, and he had tied a red rag around his arm. Both would have made the man stand out in a Saigon crowd. Fetterman could see that the man's hair had a razor cut, which suggested he was an NVA soldier. However, there was nothing on his body to identify him as such.

Fetterman picked up the weapon, the spare magazines and the grenades, leaving the dead man where he was. The master sergeant returned to the stairs and descended rapidly. He met no one. The main floor corridor was deserted, too. He left the building and hurried across the street. As he reached that side, Gerber joined him.

"What you got?"

"NVA sniper," said Fetterman.

Gerber looked up at the rooftop. He turned to speak, but there was a roar behind him. Without thinking, he dived to the street, rolling toward the wall of the closest building. Fetterman was an instant quicker.

The enemy rocket rumbled overhead and slammed into a building down the block. There was a tremendous explosion, and debris rained down, striking the street near them like flat raindrops.

Gerber raised his head. The front of a building seemed to have collapsed into the street. The interior was burning ferociously, the yellow flames curling around the upper ledge on the roof and climbing into the night sky. There were people lying in the street and more running and shouting. A siren wailed somewhere, but didn't come closer.

With that, the tempo of the city changed. It was no longer a city awake in celebration, but one alert for danger. People were no longer shouting in joy, but were screaming in panic. Many who had been dancing in the street were now running away, hoping to reach their homes and families before another enemy rocket killed them.

Fetterman got to his knees and brushed at the front of his fatigue jacket. "I don't suppose we need to head over to MACV now."

"No," said Gerber, agreeing. "I'm certain they were going to tell us that the enemy is going to attack. But we know that now."

He dropped again as another rocket exploded, this one farther away. It was a quiet roar, not like the flat, loud bang of the one moments before.

"What should we do now?" asked Fetterman.

"I think we'd better get to the embassy. There's a helipad on the roof. We can use that to get out of the city."

LE TRAN OPENED THE FIRST of the coffins carefully, hoping that the various groups had read their maps correctly. She didn't want to look in on the decomposing body of a recently dead Vietnamese. Using a crowbar taken from the group of tools hanging behind her, she strained and pushed until the lid popped up.

The men standing around her gasped in unison, and she was afraid that the mistake had been made. But then she saw the RPG-7s, grenades and satchel charges—over two hundred pounds of explosives to be directed against the American pigs.

She stepped back and let the men crowd forward. All were dressed the same: white shirts buttoned to the collar and small red rags tied around their arms. She had changed to a white blouse and black shorts.

"Don't stand there gaping," she said. "Open the other coffins."

One of the men took the crowbar from her and dropped to his knees. He levered the crowbar into the crack and pushed. There was a splitting of wood as the lid snapped open, revealing AK-47s and spare magazines—two dozen weapons, cleaned and ready to go.

Le Tran moved out of the pool of light so that she was concealed in the shadows of the auto repair shop. She stayed away from the pit where the mechanics worked under the cars. To her left was a long, low wooden table littered with oil-smeared tools, rags, auto parts, empty boxes that were covered with English, and a variety of cans. In front of her were two cars and a truck that would carry her assault force to the American embassy, and in front of the vehicles were the metal garage doors. They were closed and locked now.

"Everyone take a weapon," she ordered.

At first the men stood around the coffin like kids around a counter of free candy. Her words didn't spur them to immediate action. Then one man, his face hidden in shadows, knelt and lifted an AK out carefully, as if afraid it would break. Without waiting for orders, he grabbed one of the chest pouches, took a magazine and loaded his weapon. There was a loud, metallic sound as the bolt slipped home, stripping a round from the top of the magazine.

The men moved quickly then. First, each took a weapon, then they moved to the other coffin, picking up the equipment and loading it into the cars and the truck. They broke the loads into three separate groups so that the loss of one vehicle wouldn't mean the raid had to be aborted.

Before they climbed into the vehicles, Le Tran moved in front of them. She glanced at each face, knowing that some of them would be dead before the sun rose. She felt sadness at that, but she also felt joy. In a few hours the Americans would feel the sting of war as they had never felt it. She wanted to tell the men that they were about to embark on a great adventure. They were going to participate in something that would be talked about for centuries to come. What she wanted to do was give them a pep talk.

But then she saw the grim determination in each of the faces. There was a set of the jaw, a compressed line of bloodless lips and a hardness in the eyes. These weren't men who needed a pep talk. They just needed the order to go. They needed to begin the mission.

Still she hesitated, trying to think of something momentous to say, something to be recorded and repeated throughout history, but there was nothing there. No great line. No great thought. In the end, she just said, "Let's get going."

She turned and walked to the front of one of the cars. She waited as two men got in the back while a third threw equipment into the trunk. Then he opened one of the garage doors, hauling it up with a noisy rattling.

The small convoy left the garage. They didn't bother to close the doors or turn off the lights because they wouldn't be returning there. They entered the streets, which were becoming deserted as the people, exhausted by the Tet celebrations or frightened by the sudden violence, fled for their homes.

Ahead of them, they heard a couple of sirens as an American MP jeep raced by. It was followed by two fire trucks that seemed to be out of control, heading into the interior of the city.

Le Tran and her men slowed and turned onto Thong Nhut Boulevard on their way to the American embassy. In the distance was the boom of countermortar artillery and the detonation of rockets.

Le Tran smiled to herself. The battle was beginning.

16

SONG BE SPECIAL
FORCES CAMP

Bromhead abandoned the fire control tower, leaving his heavy weapons specialist to direct the fire of the camp's mortars. The fire support bases were withdrawing their weapons one by one as more enemy assaults were reported. Each of the bases reported that small numbers of the enemy were probing the wires outside their camps.

Bromhead had seen the enemy assault forming in the jungle north of the camp. They filtered through the trees, failing to conceal themselves. The flashes from the firing mortar tubes gave them away.

Now Bromhead was in a bunker on the northern wall, near one of the protrusions of the star-shaped camp. It was a small bunker, the floor made of thick planks and the walls created out of sandbags. A firing port in the front overlooked the empty fields and there was a door to the rear. An M-60 was sited on one side so that the men could use their M-16s on the other. In the bunker with him was a crew of highly trained Montagnards whose only real desire was to kill Vietnamese. None of them cared whether the Vietnamese they killed were from the north or the south as long as they were Vietnamese.

Bromhead used the binoculars that had been stored in the bunker to observe the enemy soldiers in the bush. He had yet to point them out to the men with him. Instead, he held the field phone to one ear. The system connected all the bunkers to the main switchboard in the commo bunker.

"I want four rounds, HE, dropped six hundred meters north of camp, bearing, zero one zero degrees."

There was an acknowledgment, and moments later, an explosion in the deep grass in the north. The rounds were short and Bromhead requested an adjustment. When it looked as if they were falling among the enemy, he shouted, "On target. Keep them coming."

And as the mortars began to rain down on the enemy, there was a rising shout from outside the camp, joined by bugles and whistles. As one, the enemy surged forward, keeping low to use the tall grass as cover.

Bromhead squeezed the handset of the field phone again, blew into the mouthpiece and said, "I want flares over the camp. Now."

Seconds later there was a pop overhead as the first of the flares went off. It was followed by another and another until the ground outside of the wire was nearly as bright as daylight. The light was yellowish and the shadows danced under the swinging flares. But now the enemy stood out as they rushed the wire.

Bromhead dropped the handset and grabbed his M-14. He aimed at the attacking soldiers as they popped up and disappeared in the grass. He watched them for a moment, but he didn't shoot. Around him was the rattling of small-arms fire. There were ruby-colored tracers flashing into the night, some of them bouncing across the open ground or tumbling into the sky.

From the enemy came a raging shout, and they opened fire. The muzzle-flashes sparkled in the grass like fireflies. There was a single, crashing explosion as part of the perimeter wire blew up. Debris and dirt rained on the bunker line as the enemy attacked. They ran forward, appearing suddenly among the strands of wire.

One squad broke off, diving for cover, and another section of the perimeter exploded. The enemy concentrated their attack, filtering it toward the base of one of the stars.

Bromhead saw what was happening. He turned and aimed at the oncoming soldiers, shooting as each target appeared. When the bolt of his weapon locked back, he dropped the magazine onto the hard wooden floor of the crowded bunker. He snatched up another, and as he reloaded, he realized how hot it was. The air inside the bunker was stifling. It reeked of sweat and fear and burnt gunpowder.

The strikers with him were working to keep the machine gun firing. The M-60 chattered, ejecting the hot brass so that it bounced off the sandbags, stinging the defenders.

As Bromhead aimed again, there was a shattering explosion only a few feet from him. The concussion knocked him to the side, slamming him into the sandbags. He lost his weapon and the bunker filled with smoke and dust. Around him he could hear the men coughing, one of them throwing up so that a new odor was added to the others.

Bromhead scrambled to the left on all fours as he searched for his rifle. He was no longer aware of the heat or the smoke or how much his eyes stung. Coughing, he ran his hands over the rough, dirty floor, cutting them on splinters or burning them on the hot brass. But he found his weapon and turned as an arm appeared at the firing port. He didn't aim. He pulled the trigger and felt the weapon jerk in his hands. From outside came a scream of pain and then another explosion. This one wasn't as loud or as deadly as the first.

Bromhead rubbed his eyes and blinked at the night. He fell back to the entrance of the bunker and found one of the strikers crouched there. The man's face was wet with blood, and he was mumbling something over and over. Bromhead grabbed him and tossed him out into the night, and then followed.

As he cleared the bunker, there was another explosion in it and smoke and dust boiled out the door. Bromhead turned and saw an enemy soldier standing in front of it. Again he fired and saw the man lifted from his feet.

He shook his head then. The cooler air outside seemed to revive him. He felt the sweat trickling down his sides. His uniform felt clammy, as if he had been swimming in tepid water.

He leaped to the left, using the bunker for protection, and searched for the enemy. Now he heard the firing from the other strikers as the VC and NVA attacked into a cross fire. There were shouts and screams. The enemy's bugles blew. Grenades exploded all around and trip flares continued to burst.

Bromhead emptied his weapon into a squad of attackers. Two of them went down. When his bolt locked back, Bromhead dropped to the ground. Sitting with his back against the ripped and leaking sandbags, he put his head down, feeling tired, feeling as if he had run a race in hundred-degree weather wrapped in wet towels. His breath rasped in his throat and burned his lungs. Around him it sounded as if the earth were destroying itself.

Without realizing it, he pulled the spent magazine from his rifle and slammed a fresh one home. He turned, got to his knees and aimed. But there were no enemy soldiers close to him. They were fleeing into the tall grass. Their weapons had ceased to fire.

Bromhead leaped to his feet and ran south. He passed a burning hootch and a sandbagged bunker that was a smoking ruin and ran over the debris from a hundred mortar hits. When he reached the bottom of the fire control tower, he stopped. He glanced up at it, at the ladder that left him exposed to enemy snipers, and hesitated. Finally he slung his weapon and scrambled up the ladder. He dived over the sandbags. He lay there for a moment panting, trying to catch his breath. When he got to his hands and knees, he saw the grinning face of his heavy weapons man.

"What's the status?"

"Lost some bunkers on the north to enemy fire. Crew-served weapons and mortars are still intact. Heavy casualties on the north, but light elsewhere."

"Situation?"

"Hell, Captain, I thought you knew. The little fuckers have turned tail."

SANTINI JOINED MADDEN in the Fifth Special Forces Headquarters. For a moment Madden stayed where he was, listening to the sound of the mortars falling and to the wail of the incoming warning horn. When he saw Santini, he snapped his fingers for attention. "What's it like out there?"

"People running all over the place with no one sure what's going on. We've taken some wounded and some killed in the mortar attacks."

"Think we should get out to the perimeter?" asked Madden.

"I don't know, sir."

"Hell, man, you were out there. You've seen the situation. Now I know they can't overrun the base—it's too big—but they could penetrate the wire and create havoc."

Santini entered the major's office and dropped onto the couch. He leaned his head against the plywood wall and closed his eyes. For an instant the scene outside the club replayed itself. He saw men falling. Men dying.

He was tired. He felt the sweat drip, and if he paid attention he could smell himself. He ached all over, the result of hitting the floor and having men land on him as they tried to find cover. Being a soldier assigned to the big base had slowed him down. He hadn't expected the enemy to hit them, and yet he knew they would because the girl had told him they would. Hell, all the signs were there.

At least he had gotten her off Nha Trang and out of the clutches of the local Vietnamese. Had he failed to do that, she would probably be dead now. He knew that the Vietnamese interrogators would kill the prisoners in retaliation for the attack tonight. He had saved her. He hoped he wouldn't be sorry he had.

"Sergeant," said Madden, "I think it's time we acted like soldiers."

Santini opened an eye and saw the major standing next to his desk. He had donned a flak jacket and a steel pot. In his right hand he held a CAR-15. Santini couldn't help laughing.

"You going to a costume party?"

Anger flashed across Madden's face and then he laughed. "Yeah, I am. Local CO has decreed that we all wear our flak jackets and steel pots."

"And you suddenly got the urge."

Madden took off his helmet and set it on the desk. "Why don't you get your weapon and we'll go find ourselves a place on the line?"

Santini forced himself to stand. He returned to his own office and grabbed the flak jacket that he had stuffed into the bottom of a filing cabinet. Then, after finding his helmet and getting his rifle, he looked into the major's office and said, "I'm all set to go."

They left the building together. Madden thought about taking a jeep, but decided it was the last thing they needed. For a moment they stood in the darkness, listening to the sounds around them: firing on the perimeter, outgoing artillery and the wail of sirens all over the compound.

Madden stopped at the corner of the building and looked back to the east. He could see the glow of fires in the distance. Jets roared from the runway and choppers popped their rotors as they got airborne, going out on countermortar.

But there was nothing coming in. There were no explosions on the base, other than rounds cooking off in the fires. There were no more mortars or rockets falling on them.

"I think they've stopped," said Santini.

"Yeah," agreed Madden. "Just harassment to let us know they're thinking of us. I'll bet some of the camps are really catching hell."

"Yes, sir."

Madden turned and ran back to one of the jeeps. He set his weapon in the back where it would be easy to retrieve. As Santini climbed into the passenger's seat, Madden said, "I doubt we're needed on the perimeter. I think we'd better head over to the TOC and see if we can make radio contact with the camps. See if there's anything they need.''

''You think they're the real targets?'' asked Santini, afraid that he'd gotten the girl out of the frying pan and into the fire.

Madden reached down to turn the ignition switch and then sat up, the engine running. ''No,'' he said, ''I don't. I think they'll take harassment fire, too, but if this is as widespread as we suggested it would be, the targets will be Vietnamese—the provincial capitals, Hue, Saigon and Da Nang—with only a few pushes at American bases.''

For some reason Santini found that estimate comforting. He relaxed, feeling the tension drain from him as if he had just learned that a tumor was benign. He closed his eyes as the major pulled out of his slot, opening them once as they hit a pothole and again when he heard shouting to one side. Then they were at the TOC and there wasn't time to relax or worry. He was busy with the radios, learning that the attacks were widespread but the casualties and damage light.

IN THE DARKENED CITY ROOM Hodges and the boys were crowded around the hammering teletype machine, sure that they were all going to die sometime before sunrise. Horrified, they watched the list of attacks grow. The teletype told them of losses at Hue, Quang Tri and Da Lat. They tried to make some sense out of it because there was so much going on.

Hodges finally tired of standing in front of the machine and reading the lines as they were printed. The tiny light above the machine tended to wash out the ink, making it hard to see. And the ribbon needed changing, but no one wanted to shut down the machine long enough to do it. They were forced to read the faint words.

Hodges collapsed into a chair and leaned an elbow on the table so that he could hold his head up with his hand. His fingers dug at his scalp as if trying to get rid of an itch. Occasionally he would sigh and say, ''God, this is terrible. For the American Army to take a beating like this. I never thought I'd see it.''

"They're holding their own," ventured Crown. "I mean, the losses all seem to be Vietnamese."

"You don't understand," moaned Hodges. "You don't understand. The enemy was defeated, everyone said so, and now suddenly, out of nowhere, there he is. Thousands of them."

Crown looked at the editor and wanted to shout at him. He remembered Morrow standing in the city room only hours earlier, telling Hodges that something was brewing. But the editor and all the others wouldn't listen. They'd seen and heard only what they'd wanted to see and hear. Now their preconceived notions were blowing up around them.

"This is worse than Custer at the Little Big Horn," said Hodges. "Christ."

"But..."

Hodges suddenly snapped up, staring. It was almost as if he had seen the headlines on the newspapers after the Custer massacre and realized that it was a hell of a story. The defeat of the American Army by a third, hell, a fifth-rate power.

"We'd better get out in the street and get some things nailed down," he said. "I want someone over at the embassy and I want someone to backstop Morrow at MACV. I want someone at Tan Son Nhut."

"What are we going to write?" asked one of the reporters.

"Use your head, man," said Hodges. "We've got a hell of a story here. Shocked people in the street. The American Army retreating all over South Vietnam. This is stacking up as a major defeat."

"Maybe we'd better let things settle down before we decide that," said Crown.

"We're not deciding anything." Hodges moved to the teletype machine and pointed at the paper rolling through it. "The enemy has already decided it. We've got to cover it. Get out there and see how badly we've been hurt."

"Maybe we should wait to see how our boys respond," tried Crown again.

"Man, you just don't get it, do you? This is a major setback for us. I don't like it, but it's a story that we've got to print.

We'd better get on it." He grabbed at the paper in the teletype, reading about more disaster in South Vietnam. "I don't like it at all," he repeated, but there was a smile on his face.

17

THE STREETS OF
SAIGON

Morrow stood in a doorway and watched the people around her. Something had changed subtly in the past few minutes. There was no longer an air of celebration. It had become an air of panic. Fright was evident on the faces of men and women as they scrambled for cover. The bursts of machine gun fire and firecrackers that had marked the party were now things to fear. Snipers seemed to be everywhere, taking shots at the people in the streets. Rockets and mortars were falling sporadically and people were dying.

The streets, which had been filled with celebrants, were rapidly becoming deserted. Around her there were men and women hiding, watching and waiting. Occasionally someone would scamper from cover, and if there were no shots, more people would run. But then the sniper would shoot again, and everyone would dive into doorways or behind cars or dodge down an alley.

In the distance more firing erupted. At first it was only a couple of weapons and then the tempo increased until it sounded as if a major firefight was developing. Morrow moved from the doorway to the sidewalk, looking in the direction of the shooting, but she couldn't see anything.

Instead of running down the street she ducked back into the shadows and then crouched. Feeling tired, sick and scared, she pressed her face against the rough stone wall of the building. Sweat stained her khaki-colored jumpsuit, but it wasn't from the heat and humidity of the night.

She realized that she was badly frightened, just as she had been several times since her arrival in Vietnam. First there had been the men forcing their way into her room in Hong Kong and then there had been the VC and NVA who had overrun Camp A-555. Men who had beaten her badly for no apparent reason. Men who felt that she was an enemy because she was an American.

Morrow closed her eyes and pushed herself into the corner and let the fear take control. She didn't want to get out of the corner. There was nothing she could do anyway. Nothing she could see and nothing to report on. For the moment the enemy didn't know where she was and she was safe. She should have taken the trip home when she'd had the chance, but she'd had to prove how brave she was.

At that moment she didn't feel brave. She felt her legs shaking and wished she was with Gerber and Fetterman. They would protect her. Every time she'd gotten into trouble they'd gotten her out of it. They'd been late doing it, but they had eventually arrived. Except that this time they didn't know where she was and she wasn't sure where they were. They had been in Saigon that afternoon, but given the circumstances they could be anywhere by now.

The panic she felt was beginning to grip her completely. She whimpered once. The sound was alien to her. It was like that of a lost puppy, like that of a person who'd lost the ability for rational thought. She took a deep, slow breath and forced herself to open her eyes.

The scene before her hadn't changed. The lights in the building across the street were out, but the neon signs still burned. The multicolored lights gave the street scene an unnatural look. Skin was blue and green, and the blood from the body sprawled in the center of the street was black.

She knew she couldn't stay where she was. She had to get moving. In her mind she could see herself on her feet, sliding along the front of the buildings, slipping out of danger. But she couldn't bring herself to get up. She wanted to, desperately, but her muscles wouldn't respond.

Then, as she concentrated on it, she realized she was on her feet. She hadn't been aware that she had stood, but suddenly she was on the street, her back pressed against the stone building. There was a man lying there, and Morrow thought he was hiding until she realized that half his head was missing. She stepped over him and hurried on until she came to a corner. The cross street was dark. Without thinking, she turned down it.

The firing that she'd heard was behind her now. She knew that as a reporter she should head toward the sound of the guns, but she didn't want to. She wanted to find somewhere she could feel safe. She wanted out of the battle before it developed into something more than the scattered snipers and small firefights.

She stopped, hiding behind a huge palm tree, searching the street in front of her. From the right there came a shattering blast and a burst of machine gun fire. Small arms erupted all around, and she knew that the American embassy was under attack. It wasn't far from where she stood.

LE TRAN HAD HER HIT SQUAD abandon their vehicles down the block, away from the wall of the American embassy. When she stepped into the street, there were only a dozen or so people milling around, waiting and watching. She pulled the .45 taken from the body of the American MP, thumbed the hammer back and pulled the trigger twice, firing into the air. The people scattered, disappearing immediately.

The men with her jumped from the truck and climbed out of the cars. They grabbed the equipment and then, without orders, split into small groups as they spread out. Le Tran whipped a red cloth from her pocket and laid it across her upper arm. With her free hand, she looped it once, caught an end in her teeth and formed a knot. Satisfied that she could now be identified as a Vietcong soldier, she joined the group of men who carried the small rocket launcher.

Hugging the shadows, they worked their way down the wide palm-lined boulevard until they were opposite the wall that ran around the embassy. Le Tran held up a hand and the men scattered, taking the little cover they could find. She waited until everyone on the assault team was in place, then touched the shoulder of the man with the rocket launcher.

He glanced over his shoulder to make sure no one was in the way of the backblast and then aimed at the wall. He pulled the trigger and rocked to the rear as the weapon fired.

Across the street the rocket slammed into the wall and exploded. There was a mushrooming of smoke and dust and a flash of bright orange light. Debris sprayed back toward them, bouncing on the street and flipping up into the air. The roar of the detonation washed out all other sound.

As soon as the smoke cleared, Le Tran was on her feet, running across the street. She dived onto the ground, crawled forward rapidly and peeked over the smoking lip of the hole. Through it was more rubble from the wall. There were palm trees, a stone fountain and bushes covered with flowers.

She was joined by two of the sappers. One turned, looked and then dived through the hole into the embassy grounds. The second man followed, and as Le Tran watched, the rest of her sapper squad entered the embassy grounds and spread out.

The first man to reach the fountain was shot at. He rolled up against the side of the fountain, then fired at a window, waited and fired again. A burst ripped up the ground in front of him and chipped stone from the fountain, covering him with a fine dust.

While the one man kept the Americans pinned down, the rest of the sappers infiltrated, slipping through the hole in the embassy wall and spreading out. Some used the bushes or palm trees as cover. Others slid along the wall until they were at the corners and then ran across the grass, hoping to penetrate either the main embassy building or into any of the other structures on the four acres.

As soon as all of the men were through the wall, Le Tran followed them. She ran toward the fountain and dropped to the ground behind it, her AK-47 clutched in her hands. Using her elbows and her knees, she worked her way around the fountain until she could see the window where one of the Americans hid. There was a flicker of movement behind it and then the flashes of the muzzle as the American put a burst into the side of the fountain. She grinned as she returned the fire.

LOCKRIDGE WAS ALONE in his corner of the embassy when part of the wall near the street blew up. In his fatigues and steel pot, he was standing near a window when it happened. He saw the flash, the orange-yellow fireball and the cloud of dust and smoke. The window shattered, and the glass fell onto the floor.

He dived to the side, his heart in his throat. His chest was thumping spasmodically under his flak jacket as he tried to figure out what had happened. There was a single burst of firing from a machine gun and then small arms. Lockridge got onto his hands and knees and crawled away from the window and broken glass, moving toward the door. Without thinking, he made sure it was locked.

He moved back toward the window and glanced out of it, staying to the side so that he would be hard to see. The embassy grounds in front of him seemed to be empty. No one was moving, but someone was shooting. There were rifle shots and bursts from automatic weapons.

Lockridge ducked and crawled under the window to look out the other side. Still nothing. Only a hole in the wall, but no one around it. Lockridge wondered if someone hadn't just tried to blow up part of it as a gesture of defiance. No one to enter, just proof that the American embassy in downtown Saigon could be a target if someone wanted it to be.

There was movement in the courtyard, near the big, round fountain. Lockridge raised his rifle, but before he could fire someone else did. He saw the tracers strike the stone and bounce off. There was a pinging sound as they ricocheted. The man crawling there returned fire.

Lockridge aimed into the middle of the muzzle-flashes and opened up. He held his finger on the trigger until it ached and the bolt of his weapon locked back, then he ducked and let the empty magazine fall to the floor. When he popped up again, there was no movement and no muzzle-flashes.

For several long minutes Lockridge searched the grounds outside his window. Overhead, there were flares bursting, throwing light onto the scene. The shifting light didn't help matters because it put the whole landscape into motion. He tried to separate the moving shadows from the VC who were out there somewhere.

Finally he spotted something that he was sure was an enemy soldier. Aiming at it, the sights of his weapon on the middle of the shape, he pulled the trigger, putting a five-round burst into it.

Immediately there was answering fire. AK rounds slammed into the wall near him. The remaining glass in the window exploded. Lockridge could hear the bullets snap as they passed close to his head, but he refused to duck. He tried to spot the enemy's weapons, but the muzzle-flashes were invisible. Fearing he was going to be killed, he dropped down and leaned against the wall, certain that he could feel the bullets hitting the other side of it.

KEEPING TO THE DARK, deserted streets, Gerber and Fetterman made good time. They trotted along the fronts of the buildings, stopping at the cross streets to make sure no one was lying in ambush. Then they rushed to seek cover on the other side. They kept the pace quick as they moved through the debris-strewn streets. Fires were burning on some blocks and cars had been overturned on others. It looked as if riots had broken out around them.

They came to a wide palm-lined boulevard. There were no lights. Overhead were the flares being dropped from aircraft or fired into the air by artillery. It was a half-light that shifted and shimmered, but it was bright enough for them to see a jeep pulled to the side of the road. The M-60 mounted in the back pointed at the sky and there seemed to be one man leaning against the front tires.

Fetterman eased toward Gerber and nodded in the direction of the jeep. "Wounded?"

"Or dead." Gerber pointed to the right and signaled him forward. When Fetterman started off, Gerber dodged to the right so that he was next to the short stone wall topped by an iron fence.

Carefully, watching the ground around them with one eye on the buildings across the street, they worked their way to the jeep. They approached it from the rear, their weapons ready. In front of it was the body of one man, his helmet on the ground next to his head as if he had set it there.

Fetterman stopped near the base of a palm, his weapon aimed in the general direction of the jeep. The man there moved his head slightly, almost as if he had heard Fetterman's approach.

When Gerber caught up, Fetterman asked, "Sir?"

"Let's check them. I'll cover."

Fetterman dropped to his stomach and crawled the last few feet to the jeep. As he reached the rear tires, he got to his feet, still crouching so that his head was below the back of the jeep. He duckwalked forward and put a hand on the man leaning against the front tire.

Slowly the man turned and grinned. There was blood on his flak jacket and on his face. He was sitting with his legs straight out in front of him, his hands at his sides, the backs resting on the ground. In his right hand was a .45, but he didn't seem to have the strength to lift it.

"Where you hit?"

The man continued to grin. His teeth were bloodstained.

Fetterman moved closer and put a hand on the man's head. His hair was clotted with blood, and Fetterman wondered if the skull had been penetrated. A bullet in the head could do strange things while a man waited to die. But there was no evidence of a hole. Just a crease in the scalp that was deep enough to have dazed him.

"My partner?"

Fetterman looked up and saw Gerber working his way to the other man. He waited as Gerber checked the body and then shook his head.

"Partner's dead," said Fetterman. "Sorry."

"He was a good kid. Fresh, and a smartass, but a good kid. Shit."

"You going to be all right?"

"I'm fine. Got a headache and can't see shit. There's three or four of you and you all keep spinning around."

"You've got a concussion and who knows what else."

"You sure my partner's dead?"

Fetterman watched Gerber drag the body out of the street and rest it against the curb. He could tell by the way the body moved as Gerber dragged it that the man was dead. There was something about the way they moved—a loose-boned shifting that a living body couldn't match. It was as if dowels had been sewn into clothes to help give them shape. Once you'd seen it, you didn't forget it.

"I'm afraid so," said Fetterman.

"Shit. He was a good kid."

"Listen, is there anything I can do for you?"

"The radio is still working. I hear it sometimes. You could call this in."

Fetterman stood up long enough to grab the microphone. He turned the gain knob and heard a burst of static, and then the air was filled with voices—nervous voices calling for help, frightened voices demanding help, quiet voices telling the others to calm down.

"Call sign is Waco. Waco One Two. Tell them we're down and need help."

Fetterman nodded and waited until there was a break in the traffic. He keyed the mike and said, "Waco Control, Waco Control, this is Waco One Two."

"One Two, say message. Quit wasting time."

"One Two is down. One dead. One wounded. Needs assistance."

There was a pause and then, "Say location."

Fetterman gave it to Waco Control. He was told that assistance was on the way. A few minutes later he heard the faint wailing of sirens. In the distance the revolving red lights reflected off the fronts of buildings.

Gerber moved toward him. "Guy took a round right between the eyes. Couldn't have known what hit him."

Fetterman looked at the man leaning on the tire. The sound from the sirens was getting closer. He said, "You're going to be okay now."

As the first of the MP jeeps skidded to a halt, Fetterman got to his feet. Gerber moved with him as a sergeant wearing a flak jacket, a steel pot instead of the normal polished helmet liner and an armband with MP on it leaped from the passenger's side.

"What happened here?"

"Ambush," said Gerber. "You've one dead and one wounded. Should get the wounded man to the hospital."

The MP crouched near the wounded man and asked, "What happened?"

"VC were waiting. Opened fire. I got hit and fell out of the jeep. I didn't see what happened to John."

In the distance there was an explosion. Everyone hit the ground. There was a burst of small-arms fire and then sporadic shooting.

"Sounds like it's close to the embassy," said the MP sergeant.

"We were heading in that direction," said Gerber. "Want to give us a lift?"

"Cruz, you and Martinez head over to the embassy and see what's happening there. I'll take Davis to the hospital." He looked at Gerber and said, "You can ride with one of them."

Cruz turned and ran to his jeep. As he grabbed the wheel, he shouted, "Let's go!"

Fetterman followed Gerber as he swung himself into the rear of the jeep. He looked at the M-60 but didn't stand behind it.

However, when Cruz slammed the jeep into gear and he was rocked to the rear, he held on to the machine gun's support.

Over the roar of the wind, Gerber yelled, "The next few minutes are going to be real interesting."

18

THE AMERICAN
EMBASSY, SAIGON

Lockridge crouched in the darkness in the ruined ground floor. He walked around, peering out windows, looking for the enemy. Occasionally he could hear them, along with firing from inside the compound. The latter came from other Marines shooting at the sappers who were trying to get inside the building.

He took up his position at the window again, searching for the enemy. Feeling the tension, he held his weapon in both hands, his fingers locked on it. The muscles of his arms were cramping with the strain, but Lockridge didn't care. He was nervous and afraid and alone, and he was convinced that he wasn't going to let anyone enter the building unless they were Americans.

Outside there was movement. Lockridge threw his weapon to his shoulder and aimed. He pulled the trigger, felt the weapon fire, then looked and saw someone scramble for cover. He fired again.

Return fire slammed into the wall near him, splattering him with chipped stone and bits of brick. Lockridge ducked, crawled under the window and popped up again, staring into the half-light outside the building. Smoke was drifting in from the north, obscuring the fountain.

There was a VC in the bushes near the wall. Lockridge was sure of it. He aimed and fired, waited and fired again. When there was no return fire, he ducked under the window so that he could look out the other side. A man was up and running—a man wearing a white shirt and black pants and carrying an AK-47. Lockridge knew that none of the Marines would be outside the buildings and that any help that arrived would not be armed with the Communist weapons. He opened fire.

The man almost reached cover. One round hit him in the shoulder and spun him around. He lost the grip on his weapon, tossing it to the ground, then rolled once as he hit the dirt and tried to stand. Lockridge aimed carefully and put a bullet into the VC's head. There was a splash of blood and the man collapsed. He didn't move.

Lockridge turned his back to the wall and slid to the floor. He held his M-16 in both hands, the butt on the floor and the muzzle pointed at the ceiling. It was the first man he had killed. The first one that he had watched die. For a moment he was sickened by what he had done, and then suddenly he was elated. He had shot an enemy soldier who would have killed him if given the chance.

Instead of worrying about it, Lockridge got to his knees and looked out the lower corner of the window. All around there was shooting. Chicom grenades were popping and shrapnel was rattling against the side of the building.

Lockridge looked around again. He had shoved the desks, chairs and tables against the doors that led into the room. He had pushed the filing cabinets into the center of the room to give himself a nest if he needed it. Papers, files, cans, pencils, maps and dozens of other small things littered the floor. The windows were broken and the air conditioner was roaring, trying to cool the room. The humidity of the early morning was seeping in. Lockridge was covered with a light coating of moisture that was nervous sweat. His skin itched.

THE JEEPS STOPPED SHORT of the embassy grounds. Gerber and Fetterman leaped out of the back and crouched, trying to figure out what was happening. There was shooting all over the embassy grounds. A machine gun nest manned by Americans had been established on the roof.

"Now what?" asked Fetterman.

Gerber shrugged. He noticed the hole blown in the wall and wondered why someone would go to that much trouble. The gate was the weakest point and could probably have been penetrated with little or no noise. Blowing a hole in the wall would alert everyone inside.

Gerber stood and took a step into the street. There was a single burst of fire from inside the compound. The bullets struck the concrete, bouncing and whining into the night. Gerber dived back for cover.

"Shit. Didn't expect that."

Fetterman scrambled around to the left so that he was on the side of the jeep opposite the embassy. He peeked over the seats, but couldn't see anything other than the wall, the tops of trees and the upper stories of the embassy. From inside came plenty of shooting, but it was single-shot or short bursts of assault rifles.

Gerber joined him. "I believe it's not much more than a squad. Maybe two."

"I agree. If there were more of them, they'd have overrun the place by now."

Gerber ducked his head and looked at his watch. "It'll be light in about an hour. Maybe less. At first light we should be able to figure out what to do."

"You mean we wait?"

Gerber nodded and then crawled around the master sergeant. He saw the jeep's driver kneeling near the front, peeking around the headlights, his eyes on the embassy.

"Cruz," he hissed. "Can you check on the status?"

"Whose?"

"People inside. See if there are any reinforcements coming."

Cruz glanced at Gerber, at the embassy and then crawled into cover. He pushed by Fetterman and snagged the microphone for the radio. "Waco Control, this is Five Five."

"Go."

Before he could speak, a rocket flashed out of nowhere and hit one of the embassy walls. There was a spectacular explosion. Debris rained down and smoke began to pour from the side of the building.

"Five Five, what in hell was that?"

"Waco Control, that was an enemy rocket. We've taken no casualties here. Say status of reinforcements?"

"We have men on the way."

"Roger."

Cruz looked at Gerber, who nodded. "Yeah. On the way."

Fetterman moved to the rear again and studied the hole in the wall. He then returned and said, "We put some people in there, we might be able to take the sappers from the rear before they can get into the building."

"Hang loose, Tony."

"Excuse me, sir," whispered Fetterman, "but those people have attacked American soil now. We have to take them, or the world is going to look down on us. We let some fifth-rate guys walk all over us . . ."

Gerber wiped a hand over his face. He turned and peered over the top of the jeep. The enemy was still invisible. There was one machine gun nest on the roof, manned by Americans. From the sound of the firing, the Marines still held practically everything.

But Fetterman had a point. Embassy grounds were considered to be the soil of the country they represented. The VC had symbolically attacked the United States. The longer the enemy stayed in there, the bigger the insult. If they could kill and capture all of the enemy soldiers, then the sting would be gone.

The only problem was that he didn't know the size of the attacking force. From the indications around them, it wasn't a large force. The last thing he needed, however, was to go off half-cocked.

"Captain," said Cruz, "we'll have some people here soon. It might be wise to lie low until the reinforcements arrive."

"Captain?" pressed Fetterman.

"Tony, we're going to hang loose for a few minutes until the reinforcements arrive. Then we'll recon and see what we need to do."

"Yes, sir."

LE TRAN HID IN THE BUSHES and watched her carefully laid plan go up in smoke. They had gotten into the embassy grounds easily, but the Marines had stopped them short of the buildings. She couldn't believe it. The Marines were all soft children who chased women, drank and talked too much. How could they stop the men of the elite C-10 Sapper Battalion?

She crawled forward slowly, using the techniques she had learned long ago, being careful not to disturb the foliage, using it to hide her movements. She came to the edge of a large expanse of lawn and studied the scene.

In front of her was debris blown off the building by the rockets: chunks of rock, metal from the shutters, papers and dirt. There was one body. She couldn't tell who it was but knew it was one of her men. His white shirt and black pants were obvious. His weapon lay near his outstretched hand.

She shook herself and tried to figure it out. Lockridge had seemed such a child, a young man who had come to Vietnam with no concept of what war was. His main interest had been to see if he could get her out of her clothes, and she had made sure he would fail. The evening she had spent with him had suggested he would run when the first shots were fired.

And his friend had seemed to be no braver. From what she could learn, the whole of the embassy guard force was like them: young men who had never seen battle and who would run when the first shots were fired. Yet that wasn't what had happened. The Marines had stayed at their posts, pouring rifle fire into the sappers as they tried to get close to the embassy building, dying bravely if necessary.

There was a burst from a machine gun, and she heard the bullets snap through the leaves above her head. She ducked quickly, her face in the dirt. She could smell the earth and was reminded of the odor earlier when they had opened the grave.

She pulled back, turned and began to crawl toward the side of the building where four men were supposed to be blowing open a door. As she neared them, she saw that one was dead, his head a mess of blood and brain. The other three were shooting at the windows on the ground floor. Occasionally someone shot back at them.

Yes, the whole plan was in ruins. There would be no great VC raid into the bowels of the American embassy. The best they could hope for now was to get inside the building and set pieces of it on fire. That would let the Americans know the enemy was tough and determined. She had hoped they would be able to capture and then execute some of the female employees. That would have made quite a splash on the evening news in the United States. But it was too late for that now. All they could do was damage the building and hope for the best.

APPROXIMATELY THE SAME TIME that the MPs began arriving at the embassy, Robin Morrow found Gerber crouched behind a jeep. She crawled forward on her stomach, using the technique Bromhead had taught her when they were all together at Camp A-555.

When she was close, she asked, "So what's the story here?"

Gerber felt the blood drain from his face. "Jesus Christ, Robin, what in hell are you doing here?"

"Looking for a story."

"You've found a hell of a good one," said Fetterman. "Nice to see you, Miss Morrow."

"Thank you, Master Sergeant. What's going on here?"

Gerber wanted to pull her back out of the way, but to do that would expose her to sniper fire, if there were snipers. It seemed best to let her stay with them.

"Well," he said, "we've got some VC inside the embassy walls, but we don't have a feel for the situation yet."

"Okay. So what are you going to do?"

"I'm hoping that someone with the MPs will be in contact with someone on the inside so that we can find out exactly what's happening."

She shook her head. "The boys over at the press bureau are going bug-fuck. They think it's the end of the world. If they knew that the VC had penetrated the embassy wall—"

"That's what I said," interrupted Fetterman. "We've got to get the enemy out of there before the press arrives." He glanced at Morrow. "Present company excepted."

Gerber wanted to say something, but the MP commander crawled over and said, "Captain . . . ah . . ."

"Gerber."

"Yes. Well, sir, do you have any observations about the present situation?"

"Nothing that would be of help. I was hoping you'd be in radio contact with someone on the inside."

"I am, sir. We know the enemy's scattered around the grounds and that he hasn't penetrated any of the buildings." The MP looked at his watch. "I think we'll hit the wall in about fifteen minutes—at dawn. Shortly after that there should be an assault force landing on the roof."

"We'd like to go with you," said Gerber.

"Glad to have you, sir. I'm afraid the lady reporter will have to stay behind."

Before Morrow could protest, Gerber said, "She'll give us a chance to clear the enemy before she enters the compound."

She glared at him and amended, "As long as you don't take too long."

"Yes, ma'am," said the MP. "If you all will come with me." He led them to the rear where the two companies of MPs were staging. He showed them a map of the embassy grounds and detailed the plan for flushing the enemy from it. When he had given them a chance to ask questions, he said, "We'll go in three minutes. Let's get set."

Using the last of the darkness for cover, the men spread out, surrounding the embassy. Gerber found himself on the street opposite the hole in the wall. Fetterman was with him, as were a dozen MPs. He watched the second hand of his watch sweep around, and as soon as it touched the twelve on the last pass, he leaped up to sprint across the street.

The men strung out behind him. They fanned out along the wall, Fetterman on the other side of the hole. Gerber looked at the master sergeant and nodded. Fetterman dived through, and an instant later Gerber followed.

He found himself behind bushes. There was no one around other than Fetterman. As he crawled forward, one of the MPs came through the hole. When Gerber reached the edge of the grass, he could see the body of one of the VC lying near the fountain.

The firing was sporadic—a burst from a machine gun, single shots from rifles or pistols. Outside the embassy grounds there were detonations from rockets and mortars as VC and NVA gunners fired indiscriminately into the city.

Gerber crawled to the right, just inside the cover of the bushes, searching for the enemy soldiers. He stopped again and eased his way forward, but the grounds seemed to be empty.

The Special Forces captain retreated until he reached the wall. He stood up and extended his left hand so that he touched the rough surface. Slowly he moved west along the wall, his eyes scanning the surroundings. Although there was nothing to see, he could hear the firing. It came and went as the two sides spotted, then lost sight of each other.

Gerber stopped when he reached a corner. He crouched and, through gaps in the foliage, saw three or four VC barricaded across the parking lot. They had turned over a car and dragged a fifty-five-gallon drum and a couple dozen sandbags to it. Hidden in their makeshift bunker, they were shooting at anything that moved. Marines on the roof fired down at them, but weren't having any luck.

Gerber turned and waited for Fetterman. The master sergeant caught up, and Gerber pointed at the enemy. Fetterman nodded his understanding and slipped around Gerber, keeping low. The Special Forces captain checked his watch. The rising sun was lighting the scene for him now. Rather than a black shape spitting fire, there were individual gray shapes. A few more minutes and he would be able to see their faces.

While he waited for Fetterman, Gerber crawled forward slowly. His elbows and knees were wet now as he dragged them through the moist earth. He could smell the dirt and a sickeningly sweet odor from the flowers that were beginning to respond to the sun. Smoke drifted toward him, carrying the stench of burning flesh.

He shook himself and kept moving until he could see the enemy barricade. Then he stopped and pushed his rifle out so that he could aim. He waited as the VC shot at the Marines on the roof or poured fire into the windows of the embassy building.

One of the VC stepped back, and as he did, he exposed himself. Gerber didn't hesitate. Training his M-16's sights on the man's head, he pulled the trigger. He felt the recoil of his weapon and saw the round strike the enemy. The pith helmet the VC wore flew off in a spray of crimson as the man's head exploded.

As the VC tumbled to the ground, Fetterman dashed from hiding, dived for the rear of the car and lay still. The bullets fired by the Marines on the roof slammed into the barricade. The car rocked gently under the impact of the rounds, the large can vibrated and sandbags began to bleed sand.

Fetterman rolled onto his back, took out a grenade and pulled the pin. He hesitated, then let the spoon fly. After a pause, he tossed the grenade over the rear of the car, then rolled onto his stomach and scrambled to the rear.

An instant later there was an explosion. As the grenade detonated, Fetterman spun and leaped to his feet. He jumped to the barricade, his weapon ready, but the enemy had been killed. Looking toward the vegetation where Gerber hid, he held up a thumb.

Gerber ran over to him and dropped to a knee next to the car. He glanced over at the bodies of the dead men. All three had been shredded by the explosion and shrapnel. Their blood stained the concrete and their white shirts. Gerber turned away, not wanting to see any more. He'd seen too many dead men, their bodies obscenely ripped apart by bullets and grenades. A quick look told him that all three were dead. They couldn't be playing possum; the wounds were too severe.

One of the Marines stuck his head over the edge of the building. Fetterman held a thumb up, telling him that the site was secure now. There was still firing from other parts of the embassy grounds, but it had dropped off.

Then, overhead, came the pop of rotor blades as a single Huey dived for the rooftop helipad on the embassy building. It came almost straight down, first rolling over onto its right side and then twisting as it pulled out, the rotor blades popping heavily like a machine gun firing slowly. When it disappeared from sight, Gerber expected to hear an explosion, but that didn't happen.

"We're in good shape now," said Fetterman. "Reinforcements."

Gerber nodded as the MP captain ran up. "Guys from the 101st Airborne are landing on the roof."

"Great," said Gerber.

"Not much more to do here," he said. "We've secured most of the grounds and killed all the VC."

LOCKRIDGE SET HIS FULL magazines on the edge of a desk and counted them again. He was running out of ammunition. He had burned through too much of it too fast. That was something that no one had bothered to tell him in training. He had thought it was great that everyone had an automatic weapon and hadn't thought about the fact that holding the trigger down emptied the magazine in seconds. He could have fired all his ammo in a minute if he had worked at it.

Lockridge crossed the floor, staying low. His feet crunched the broken glass from the windows. Staying in the shadows, he looked out into the graying dawn. There was no one visible.

He moved around and looked out another window. The fountain was visible as was the body of a dead VC. There was rubble, broken bricks and pieces of stone scattered across the lawn.

Lockridge crouched and went to the last window. There was an expanse of concrete, lawn and then foliage that concealed the wall. Suddenly he saw a flicker of movement at the edge of the lawn behind the branches of a bush and the lacy leaves of a giant fern. He ducked under the window and popped up on the other side so that he could get a better look at it.

The firing from outside had tapered to almost nothing now. Farther away, from outside the embassy grounds, it sounded as if the world were ending, but inside it seemed safe. He made another quick circuit around his room, but there was nothing to see—only a couple of bodies, rubble and smoke.

LE TRAN KNEW THE ASSAULT had failed. She'd known it the moment they had failed to get into the embassy building. She had hoped they could salvage part of the mission and blow up the bottom floor, but now even that was impossible.

Staying where she was, Le Tran hid under a thornbush that ripped at her white shirt and snagged her black shorts. She moved as little as possible, watching the slow destruction of her sapper team as the American MPs methodically hunted them down and exterminated them. At least none of her men had tried to surrender. They all died fighting, and that was something.

In front of her, barricaded in the ground floor of the embassy, was a Marine. She had seen him in there as he had run from window to window. Once or twice she had tried to kill him, but he seemed to lead a charmed life.

Now there was nothing left to do. The great attack had failed and there was no way she was going to be able to get out of the embassy area alive. Too many Americans were swarming over the ground. All she could do was die in one great defiant act. She would take the Marine with her, the man who seemed to symbolize her defeat.

Before she attacked she checked her weapon one final time, making sure she had a full magazine. Carefully she slipped out of the equipment she wore, leaving the chest pouch, the pistol belt with the canteen and first-aid kit, and her knife behind her. She hid them the best she could to deny them to the

Americans, not that the rich capitalists needed the equipment. They would turn it into souvenirs to be sold to the young and unsuspecting.

Now she waited, watching the window in front of her, waiting for the Marine to show himself. There was a flicker at the window, and she knew the man was there. Without a thought she was on her feet, running forward, screaming at the top of her voice and firing her weapon as she ran. She saw the bullets striking the wall by the window, saw the last of the glass disintegrate and then saw the man—saw his face in the half-light cast by the rising sun and recognized him.

LOCKRIDGE HAD FINALLY convinced himself that he was going to live through the siege. He peered out of the window at a flicker of movement. A human shape burst from cover and ran toward him. He heard the scream, a cry of rage, and saw the weapon being fired. He heard the bullets striking the wall around him and snapping through the remains of the glass.

Instinctively he raised his weapon and aimed. As his finger tightened on the trigger, he got a good look at the face. Through the smoke and darkness, he saw that it was a woman. He knew her. He'd dated her.

He lowered his rifle and stared. He was rocked with confusion. Unsure of what to do, he stepped to the side. Staring at the dirty face, the soiled white shirt and the black shorts, he felt his stomach flip over and his head spin. The window frame beside him exploded as a round smashed into it.

Anger overwhelmed him then. She had never cared for him. Like so many others on both sides, she had been using him just as Jones had suggested. She had only wanted information.

He pressed his rifle against his shoulder, pulled the trigger and kept firing until he saw her stumble. She fell to one knee and lost her rifle. She stood up slowly, wobbling, and tried to walk. Blood spread rapidly on her white shirt and on the side of her head.

Lockridge stepped forward, his rifle pointed at her. She leaned to the side and tried to pick up her own weapon but fell to her hands and knees. She rolled onto her back, lifted one hand into the air as if to ward off a final blow, then died.

WITHIN MINUTES more helicopters landed on the roof of the embassy. When the assault force was formed, they started down, checking each of the floors as they went. There was heavy damage caused by rockets, but no evidence that the VC had penetrated the building. By 8:30 the assault force had linked up with the MPs who had attacked on the ground. The bodies of the VC, including Le Tran Duc, had been dragged into the open.

Gerber and Fetterman stayed in the rear, watching the men do their jobs, impressed with their professionalism. They cleared the embassy grounds quickly, determining that there were no more enemy soldiers around.

The press, which had been kept out until the Army and the Marines were certain the enemy threat had been eliminated, walked around in a daze. They pointed to the bodies of the enemy dead, photographed the damage and demanded to know how such a thing could happen.

Fetterman leaned close to Gerber, watching the press swarm like vultures. "They're not going to understand. They're going to think of this as a terrible defeat, never realizing that the enemy achieved none of its goals."

"You could tell them, Master Sergeant."

"No, sir. Wouldn't listen to me. It'll all hinge on how General Westmoreland handles the press briefing."

Both of them glanced up at the flagpole on the corner of the building and watched as the Marine guard raised the Stars and Stripes.

They were only five hours late.

AFTERWORD

Contrary to the belief that has been reported repeatedly in the media, Tet wasn't a defeat for the American forces in Vietnam. At least it wasn't until the press turned it into one.

As the first reports came in, members of the press, as well as members of the Administration and Congress, were stunned by the initial gains of the enemy. Within a week, with a few notable exceptions, those gains had been reversed and wiped out. The loss to the enemy, particularly the Vietcong, was enormous.

The media finally understood that Tet wasn't a military loss for the Americans. But they had to say something. They began labeling it a military victory but a psychological defeat. It wasn't a psychological defeat until they turned it into one. Even today many "history" books claim Tet as a partial victory for the enemy.

The purpose here was to explain how these views could be developed and to show the reader the danger of a press that isn't held accountable for its mistakes.

GLOSSARY

AC—Aircraft commander. The pilot in charge of an aircraft.

AFVN—U.S. armed forces radio and television network in Vietnam. Army PFC Pat Sajak was probably the most memorable of AFVN's DJs with his loud and long, "GOOOOOOOOOOOOOD MORNing, Vietnam!" The spinning Wheel of Fortune gives no clues about his whereabouts today.

AK-47—Assault rifle normally used by the North Vietnamese and the Vietcong.

AO—Area of Operations.

AO DAI—Long dresslike garment, split up the sides and worn over pants.

AP ROUNDS—Armor-piercing ammunition.

APU—Auxiliary Power Unit. An outside source of power used to start aircraft engines.

ARC LIGHT—Term used for a B-52 bombing mission. It was also know as heavy arty.

ARVN—Army of the Republic of Vietnam. A South Vietnamese soldier. Also known as Marvin Arvin.

BISCUIT—C-rations.

BODY COUNT—Number of enemy killed, wounded or captured during an operation. Used by Saigon and Washington as a means of measuring progress of the war.

BOOM-BOOM—Term used by Vietnamese prostitutes in selling their product.

BOONDOGGLE—Any military operation that hasn't been completely thought out. An operation that is ridiculous.

BOONIE HAT—Soft cap worn by a grunt in the field when he wasn't wearing his steel pot.

BUSHMASTER—Jungle warfare expert or soldier skilled in jungle navigation. Also a large deadly snake not common to Vietnam but mighty tasty.

C AND C—Command and Control aircraft that circled overhead to direct the combined air and ground operations.

CAO BOIS—Cowboys. A term that referred to the criminals of Saigon who rode motorcycles.

CARIBOU—Cargo transport plane.

CHINOOK—Army Aviation twin-engine helicopter. A CH-47. Also known as a shit hook.

CHOCK—Refers to the number of the aircraft in the flight. Chock Three is the third. Chock Six is the sixth.

CLAYMORE—Antipersonnel mine that fires 750 steel balls with a lethal range of fifty meters.

CLOSE AIR SUPPORT—Use of airplanes and helicopters to fire on enemy units near friendlies.

CO CONG—Female Vietcong.

DAI UY—Vietnamese army rank equivalent to captain.

DEROS—Date of Estimated Return from Overseas Service.

E AND E—Escape and Evasion.

FEET WET—Term used by pilots to describe flight over water.

FIVE—Radio call sign for the executive officer of a unit.

FOX MIKE—FM radio.

FNG—Fucking New Guy.

FREEDOM BIRD—Name given to any aircraft that took troops out of Vietnam. Usually referred to the commercial jet flights that took men back to the World.

GARAND—M-1 rifle that was replaced by the M-14. Issued to the Vietnamese early in the war.

GO-TO-HELL RAG—Towel or any large cloth worn around the neck by grunts.

GRAIL—NATO name for shoulder-fired SA-7 surface-to-air missile.

GUARD THE RADIO—Term meaning to stand by in the commo bunker and listen for messages.

GUIDELINE—NATO name for the SA-2 surface-to-air missile.

GUNSHIP—Armed helicopter or cargo plane that carries weapons instead of cargo.

HE—High-explosive ammunition.

HOOTCH—Almost any shelter, from temporary to long-term.

HORN—Term that referred to a specific kind of radio operations that used satellites to rebroadcast messages.

HORSE—See *Biscuit*.

HOTEL THREE—Helicopter landing area at Saigon's Tan Son Nhut Airport.

HUEY—UH-1 helicopter.

IN-COUNTRY—Term used to refer to American troops operating in South Vietnam. They were all in-country.

INTELLIGENCE—Any information about enemy operations. It can include troop movements, weapons capabilities, biographies of enemy commanders and general information about terrain features. It is any information that would be useful in planning a mission.

KA-BAR—Type of military combat knife.

Tet

KIA—Killed In Action. (Since the U.S. was not engaged in a declared war, the use of the term KIA was not authorized. KIA came to mean enemy dead. Americans were KHA or Killed in Hostile Action.)

KLICK—A thousand meters. A kilometer.

LIMA LIMA—Land Line. Refers to telephone communications between two points on the ground.

LLDB—Luc Luong Dac Biet. The South Vietnamese Special Forces. Sometimes referred to as the Look Long, Duck Back.

LP—Listening Post. A position outside the perimeter manned by a couple of people to give advance warning of enemy activity.

LZ—Landing Zone.

M-3—Also known as a grease gun. A .45-caliber submachine gun that was favored in World War II by GIs because its slow rate of fire meant the barrel didn't rise and they didn't burn through their ammo as fast as they did with some of their other weapons.

M-14—Standard rifle of the U.S. Eventually replaced by the M-16. It fired the standard NATO round—7.62mm.

M-16—Became the standard infantry weapon of the Vietnam War. It fired 5.56 mm ammunition.

M-79—Short-barreled, shoulder-fired weapon that fires a 40 mm grenade. These can be high explosives, white phosphorus or canister.

MACV—Military Assistance Command, Vietnam. Replaced MAAG in 1964.

MEDEVAC—Also called Dust-Off. Helicopters used to take wounded to medical facilities.

MIA—Missing In Action.

MOS—Military Occupation Specialty—a job description.

MPC—Military Payment Certificates. GI play money.

NCO—Noncommissioned officer. A noncom. A sergeant.

NCOIC—NCO In Charge. Senior NCO in a unit, detachment or patrol.

NEXT—The man who said it was his turn next to be rotated home. See *Short*.

NINETEEN—Average age of combat soldier in Vietnam, as opposed to twenty-six in World War II.

NOUC-MAM—Foul-smelling sauce used by the Vietnamese.

NVA—North Vietnamese Army. Also used to designate a soldier from North Vietnam.

P (PIASTER)—Basic monetary unit in South Vietnam, worth slightly less than a penny.

PETA-PRIME—Tarlike substance that melted in the heat of the day to become a sticky black nightmare that clung to boots, clothes and equipment. It was used to hold down the dust during the dry season.

PETER PILOT—Copilot in a helicopter.

PLF—Parachute Landing Fall. The roll used by parachutists on landing.

POW—Prisoner Of War.

PRC-10—Portable radio.

PRC-25—Lighter portable radio that replaced the PRC-10.

PULL PITCH—Term used by helicopter pilots that means they are going to take off.

PUNJI STAKE—Sharpened bamboo hidden to penetrate the foot. Sometimes dipped in feces.

RINGKNOCKER—Graduate of a military academy. The term refers to the ring worn by all graduates.

RON—Remain Overnight. Term used by flight crews to indicate a flight that would last longer than a day.

RPD—Soviet light machine gun 7.62 mm.

RTO—Radio Telephone Operator. The radio man of a unit.

SA-2—Surface-to-air missile fired from a fixed site. A radar-guided missile that is nearly thirty-five feet long.

SA-7—Surface-to-air missile that is shoulder-fired and has infrared homing.

SAFE AREA—Selected Area for Evasion. It doesn't mean that the area is safe from the enemy, only that the terrain, location or local population make the area a good place for escape and evasion.

SAM TWO—A reference to the SA-2 Guideline.

SAR—Search And Rescue. SAR forces would be the people involved in search-and-rescue missions.

SIX—Radio call sign for the unit commander.

SHIT HOOK—Name applied by troops to the Chinook helicopter because of all the "shit" stirred up by its massive rotors.

SHORT—Term used by a soldier in Vietnam to tell all who would listen that his tour was about over.

SHORT-TIMER—Person who had been in Vietnam for nearly a year and who would be rotated back to the World soon. When the DEROS (Date of Estimated Return from Overseas Service) was the shortest in the unit, the person was said to be next.

SKS—Soviet-made carbine.

SMG—Submachine gun.

SOI—Signal Operating Instructions. The booklet that contained the call signs and radio frequencies of the units in Vietnam.

SOP—Standard Operating Procedure.

STEEL POT—Standard U.S. Army helmet. The steel pot was the outer metal cover.

TEAM UNIFORM OR COMPANY UNIFORM—UHF radio frequency on which the team or the company communicates. Frequencies were changed periodically in an attempt to confuse the enemy.

THREE—Radio call sign of the operations officer.

THREE CORPS—Military area around Saigon. Vietnam was divided into four corps areas.

TRIPLE A—Antiaircraft Artillery or AAA. Anything used to shoot at airplanes and helicopters.

THE WORLD—The United States.

TOC—Tactical Operations Center.

TOT—Time Over Target. Refers to the time that the aircraft is supposed to be over the drop zone with the parachutists, or the target if the plane is a bomber.

TWO—Radio call sign of the intelligence officer.

TWO-OH-ONE (201) FILE—Military records file that listed all of a soldier's qualifications, training, experience and abilities. It was passed from unit to unit so that the new commander would have some idea about the capabilities of an incoming soldier.

UMZ—Ultramilitarized Zone. It was the name GIs gave to the DMZ (Demilitarized Zone).

UNIFORM—Refers to the UHF radio. Company Uniform would be the frequency assigned to that company.

VC—Vietcong, called Victor Charlie (phonetic alphabet) or just Charlie.

VIETCONG—Contraction of Vietnam Cong San (Vietnamese Communist).

VIET CONG SAN—Vietnamese Communists. A term in use since 1956.

WHITE MICE—Referred to the Vietnamese military police because they all wore white helmets.

WIA—Wounded In Action.

WILLIE PETE—WP, White phosphorus, called smoke rounds. Also used as antipersonnel weapons.

WSO—Weapons System Officer. The name given to the man who rode in the back seat of a Phantom because he was responsible for the weapons systems.

XO—Executive officer of a unit.
ZAP—To ding, pop caps or shoot. To kill.
ZIP—Derogatory term applied to the South Vietnamese.
ZIPPO—Flamethrower.

DON PENDLETON's

MACK BOLAN.

More SUPERBOLAN bestseller action! Longer than the monthly series SuperBolans feature Mack in more intricate, action-packed plots— more of a good thing.

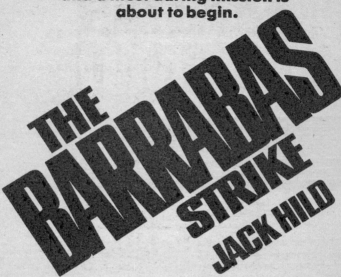

The Badlands Just Got Worse...

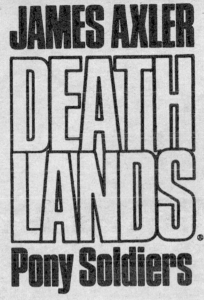

JAMES AXLER

DEATH LANDS®

Pony Soldiers

Ryan Cawdor and his band of postholocaust survivors make a
startling discovery when they come face-to-face with a spector
from the past—either they have chron-jumped back to the
1800s or General Custer has been catapulted into the twenty-
second century....